Books by Oliver Butterworth

The Enormous Egg
The Trouble with Jenny's Ear

the TROUBLE with JENNY'S EAR

the TROUBLE with JENNY'S EAR

Oliver Butterworth

Illustrated by Julian de Miskey

Little, Brown and Company

Boston   New York   Toronto   London

First Little, Brown Paperback Edition

ISBN 0-316-11922-9

Library of Congress Catalog Card Number 60-5874

10 9 8 7 6 5 4 3 2 1

MV-NY

Published simultaneously in Canada
by Little, Brown & Company (Canada) Limited

Printed in the United States of America

To my wife,

who keeps things in their place

the TROUBLE with JENNY'S EAR

CHAPTER ONE

THE PEARSON FAMILY bowed their five heads over the supper table and looked down at the tablecloth. It was white with red checks, and there were several spots around Stanley's place, because he was ten years old and a vigorous eater.

Mr. Pearson cleared his throat. "Ahem," he said. "Let us give thanks for all this good food, and our peaceful home, and our honorable state of Massachusetts, and for the fine weather we had today. It's been awfully good weather for almost November."

"And for the wonderful red leaves on our maple tree," Mrs. Pearson added.

"And for the touchdown I made at school today," Joe Pearson said, looking up from the tablecloth.

"Now just a minute," Mr. Pearson said. "It's my job to say grace, and I object to all these amendments being tacked on without my approval. If

3

someone else wants to say grace, I'll be glad to let them have a turn, and then they can put in about the leaves or the touchdowns or anything else they like. But let me say my own grace. It's the only chance I have to talk around here without being interrup—"

"Say, what's all this wire on the back of my chair?" Stanley Pearson said. "It sticks into my back."

"That's mine," Joe Pearson said. "I found it out in the tool shed. I'm going to use it for the aerial for our crystal set."

"What's the matter with Jenny?" Stanley asked, pointing across the table at his sister. She was still sitting with her head bowed, looking down at the tablecloth.

"Daddy hasn't said amen yet," Jenny said without moving her head. She was only six and had principles.

"Oh," Mr. Pearson said. "So I haven't. Amen. There, now let's have supper, for goodness' sake."

He served out the lamb stew, and they all passed the plates around until everybody had some.

"My brother Harold is coming up for supper tomorrow," Mrs. Pearson said. "He's driving up from Southwick with a new refrigerator for the Zwillingers. He said he had a surprise for you children."

4

"Oh, good," Joe said. "It's great having an uncle in the electrical business."

Stanley reached for another piece of bread. "He said he'd bring up some earphones to use with our crystal set."

"That's why we've got to get the aerial up right away," Joe said. "We want to have it all ready to work the minute we get the earphones on. We can run the aerial wire from my window right over to the maple tree—"

Mrs. Pearson put down her fork and looked at him. "Now you're not going to hang a lot of wires all over our maple tree, are you? It's *such* a nice tree, and it's so handsome just the way it is. It would be a pity to spoil it by hanging wires all over it."

"It won't be *all over* it, Mom. There's just one wire—and a couple of insulators. You'll never notice it. Honest you won't."

"Oh, you'd be surprised what I'd notice, Joe. I'm a very noticing person. I've had to be for twelve years now, ever since you were born. I noticed a bicycle pump right at the top of the cellar stairs this morning. If I hadn't noticed that I might have broken my neck."

"Oh, yes," Joe said. "I was wondering where I'd left that. We were blowing up a couple of old inner tubes down cellar. We put them in a burlap sack and pumped them up to make a tackling dummy."

"How'd it work?" Mr. Pearson asked.

"It didn't. Teddy Watson shot an arrow at it and all the air came out."

"Oh," Mr. Pearson said. No one said anything for a while after that.

"Speaking of the Watsons," Mr. Pearson said, "Jim Hagerty told me that Henry Watson was going to move his family to Florida."

"To Florida?" Mrs. Pearson said. "What will he do with all his land, do you suppose?"

"Don't know. It may all be just a rumor, anyway." Mr. Pearson stirred his coffee very slowly for a while, and looked as if he were thinking about something. "I can't imagine the town of Pearson's Corners without the Watson family in it. There have been Watsons here for just about as long as the Pearsons."

"I thought the Watsons settled here first," Joe said. "They own most of the land."

"Oh, no," his father said. "Great-great-grandfather Pearson first settled here, and they called it Pearson's Corners after him. The first Watson came to work for him, and helped him clear the land and build stone walls here, back in the 1820's. Those Watsons were great workers, and in my grandfather's day

6

they bought the Pearson farm, and Grandfather Pearson made a living as a Yankee peddler, driving around all summer in his wagon, selling pots and pans and clocks and lamp chimneys. After the Civil War Pearson's Corners got to be a small town, and grandfather set up a store at the crossroads here, and Pearson's Hardware has been the family business ever since."

"Maybe we could buy the land back again from the Watsons," Joe said. "Could we do that, Pop?"

His father shook his head. "Pearson's Hardware doesn't make that kind of money, Joe. It's about all we can do to hang on to our house here."

"Maybe Mr. Watson would give the land to us," Jenny said. "If he's going away he wouldn't want it, so he could give it to us."

"Hah!" Stanley said. "People don't *give* things away, Jenny. They just do that on those TV shows. You know, where they give you a house and a garage and a new car for remembering who the first President was."

CHAPTER TWO

UNCLE HAROLD arrived just before supper the next day. As usual, he parked his pickup truck in the back yard, and Joe and Stanley rushed out to meet him, leaving the kitchen door wide open behind them.

Uncle Harold was long and loose-jointed. A lock of sandy hair was always falling down over his eyes, and his coat pockets sagged with pliers and screwdrivers and friction tape.

"Hi, kids!" he called. "Got your antenna strung up yet?"

"Sure," Joe said. He pointed to the wire, which ran in a drooping line from his window in the back of the house over to the maple tree.

"Did you put an insulator at each end, the way I told you?"

"Yup," Joe said. "And I hooked up the antenna

wire to the tuning coil, and I fastened the ground wire to the gutter pipe, just the way you said."

"Good," Uncle Harold said. He pulled two earphones out of his pocket. "Here. This is an old set I picked out of my junk box, but they work all right. Just connect one wire to the base of the cat's whisker arm and the other to the ground connection, and you're all set. Got that?"

"Sure," Joe said, taking the earphones. He dashed across the yard into the house.

Stanley started to follow, but stopped and looked back. "Is that the surprise that Mom told us about?"

"The earphones? Heck, no," Uncle Harold said. "They're no surprise. I told you last week I'd bring them."

"Then where's the surprise? I bet I know." He started moving warily toward the truck, but Uncle Harold caught him by the tail of his jacket.

"Hold on, Stanley. Nothing doing on that till after supper. You go on in and help your brother hook up the earphones."

Stanley disappeared into the house, leaving the kitchen door open behind him. Uncle Harold lifted a carton out of the pickup truck and carried it into the kitchen.

"Hey there, Sis," he greeted Mrs. Pearson. "What's for supper? Hello, Ed, how's the hardware business?"

"Can't complain," Mr. Pearson said. "How are you getting along? People still buying deep freezers?"

"You bet. Sold two this past week. Hi there, Jenny! How are you, anyway?"

"I'm fine, Uncle Harold," Jenny said. "What's in the box?"

He looked down at the carton he was holding. "Oh, this? It's a present I brought over for the boys. It's a surprise."

Jenny carried a dish of butter out to the dining room. She came back and stood in front of her uncle and looked up at him. "Did you bring me a present too, Uncle Harold?"

Uncle Harold didn't say anything at first. He put the box down on the counter and felt around in his pockets among the fuse plugs and switches.

"Well, Jenny . . . you see, I don't usually find much around my shop that would be interesting for a girl—"

Jenny kept on looking up at him, not even blinking.

"But I did bring . . . yes, I did bring some material

to make you a pair of earrings. I just wanted to be sure about the size before I finished them."

He pulled a length of bell wire out of his left pocket and pushed back the insulation, showing a strand of gleaming copper. He took out a pair of pliers and snipped off two pieces. Then he coiled them up tightly in his long fingers, made a little loop at the ends, and bent over and squeezed one on each of Jenny's ears. She smiled and wiggled her head to feel the earrings.

"Thanks, Uncle Harold," she said and whisked out of the room. They could hear her running up the stairs. Her voice floated down from the second floor.

"There! He *did* bring me a present, after all. See, you smarties!"

Uncle Harold ran his finger around inside his collar. "Whew!" he said. "That was a close call! I'll know better next time."

His sister laughed at him. "That's just like you, Harold. You were always forgetting us girls. When you were a kid you used to go around trailing wires and buzzers and things, and all the boys would follow you around, but you never could understand why girls weren't interested in your doorbells and clock springs."

Uncle Harold rubbed his chin. "I guess you're right, Sis. Probably that's why I haven't gotten married yet. Do you suppose it's too late? I'm almost twenty-eight."

"Of course not," Mrs. Pearson said. "All you have to do is give them earrings for presents instead of the insides of alarm clocks."

"Is it that simple?" Uncle Harold said.

"Pretty near. Now the casserole's all ready, so wash up and let's have supper."

The children had to be called three times before they finally came downstairs.

"Well, kids," Uncle Harold said, reaching for the biscuits, "did the earphones work out all right?"

"Oh, sure," Joe said. "You could hear as clear as anything."

"Omms Glumpf," Stanley said. "Jome I coom—"

"*Stanley!*" his mother said. "Don't talk with your mouth full."

Stanley stretched his neck forward and forced down a huge swallow that would have strangled a grownup. "Joe and I could listen at the same time. We each held onto one earphone, and we let Jenny listen when there was only music."

"Well," Mr. Pearson said, "this is a historic moment in the Pearson house. Like the first telegraph message between Washington and Baltimore, back in the 1840's. The first words that came over the wire then were 'What hath God wrought?' What were the first words that you heard? Can you remember?"

"Sure," Joe said. "It was a kind of a song they were singing. It went like this:

> "Gumbo Pudding, rich and thick,
> Good for you, tastes so slick."

"And we could hear every word," Stanley said. "Just as if somebody were talking to you right there in the room."

CHAPTER THREE

AFTER SUPPER Uncle Harold went out to the kitchen and brought in the carton. "Now for the surprise, boys," he said. "You've done so well putting your crystal set together that I figured you could handle something a little more complicated."

The two boys peered into the box as he lifted out a long metal case with radio tubes sticking out through the top.

"It's a radio!" Joe said. "A real electric one. Maybe now we can get more than that one station."

"No, no," Uncle Harold said. "It's not a radio. It's an amplifier. A good strong one—twenty watts. That'll make enough noise for anybody."

"And what's this?" Stanley asked, looking down into the carton.

"Oh, yes. We mustn't forget that." Uncle Harold

lifted a big bowl-shaped object out of the carton. "This is the speaker."

"Oh, I know what that's for," Stanley said. "That's where the sound comes out. I bet it makes a terrific noise. Let's turn it on and hear it!"

"Hey, not so fast," Uncle Harold laughed. "It isn't as simple as all that. There wouldn't be anything to hear if you did turn it on. You see, the amplifier strengthens the radio wave, and the speaker turns it into sound, but you've got to have something to feed the radio wave into the amplifier."

"Oh," Stanley said.

"You mean you've still got to have a radio," Joe said. "Is that it?"

"Well, it all depends what you want to use it for. If you want to listen to radio programs, then you have to have a radio tuner of some kind. But that's only one thing you can do."

"What else can you do?" Stanley wanted to know. "Can you get television on it?"

"No, not television, but just about everything else. You see, this amplifier provides the power for all kinds of sound systems. With some microphones and speakers you can make an intercom for the house here, so you can talk from your room down to the kitchen, for instance, or out to the shed. Or you could have a loudspeaker out on the porch turned up full, so your mother could call you to supper. Or you could hook up a record player and play music in any room in the house, or you could play music through the outdoor loudspeaker when you were having sliding parties in the winter, or you could hook up a radio tuner and listen to programs anywhere in the house or outdoors. Or you could even hitch on a tape recorder and record what you're saying around the house, at the supper table for instance, and then you could play it back through the amplifier, and hear it anywhere you wanted, or any time you wanted. You see what you can do with it?"

Joe and Stanley were listening with their mouths open.

"Do you mean we can really *do* it?" Stanley said. "I mean, can we do *all* those things? Oh boy! Let's go! What are we waiting for?"

"Oh, cool off, Stanley," Joe said. "Didn't you hear what Uncle Harold said? He said you got to have microphones and things like that to hitch onto the amplifier. We can't do any of those things unless we get the stuff to hitch on."

"But we can get the things from Uncle Harold," Stanley said. "Can't we, Uncle Harold?"

17

"Sure, Stanley. I just didn't want to bring everything all at once, so you wouldn't get too mixed up. I've got all kinds of old microphones and speakers and record players in the shop that nobody wants, and I can't sell them, so I might as well give them to you kids."

Mrs. Pearson had been watching the three of them. "But Harold," she said, "do you really think you ought to *give* them all these things? It doesn't seem quite right, somehow. They may get to think that *everything's* going to be given to them, if they just ask for it."

Joe and Stanley turned to their mother in alarm, but Uncle Harold looked at them and smiled.

"Don't worry about that, Sis. Just look at it this way. It's just as if they found all this electrical stuff in a junk yard. If it's there and nobody wants it, and it would just have to be thrown out someday, why not let them use it? It isn't as if somebody *bought* the stuff for them. These are parts that other people have thrown away, and if the boys can do something with them, then it saves those things from being wasted. You wouldn't want it all wasted, would you, Sis?"

"Well . . . no, I guess not," Mrs. Pearson said doubtfully.

"And then think what they'll learn about electronics," Uncle Harold went on. "There's nothing like starting young this way. By the time they're in high school they'll be able to do all your electrical repairs for you. They might even become electrical engineers. Once you get kids interested in something like this, you never know where it might lead."

"Yes, I know," Mrs. Pearson said. "That's what I was wondering about."

"I think Harold's got a point there," Mr. Pearson said. "This looks like a chance for the boys to pick up a little information about radio and things like that. This electronics stuff is getting to be a pretty big thing these days. It would be handy for a young fellow to know something about it. And if the boys are interested, and if Harold's got some old parts he doesn't want—"

"Doesn't *want!*" Uncle Harold said. "Why, you ought to see my spare-parts collection. I just can't bring myself to throw anything away, and all this used stuff keeps coming in and piling up, and I don't know what to do with it all. The more that Joe and Stanley can use, the better I'd like it. Honest."

Mrs. Pearson smiled and nodded. "Well, I suppose it's all right, if you put it that way. I just don't like to think of all those spare parts cluttering up the house, and wires all over the place, and megaphones in every room—"

"Not megaphones, Mom, *microphones*," Joe insisted.

"All right, microphones, then, or whatever they are. But I suppose that's the way boys are. If I could stand growing up with an electrical brother, I ought to be able to stand a couple of electrical sons."

"That's right, Mom," Joe said. "I knew you'd see it our way. And we'll promise to keep the wires and things out of sight as much as we can so they won't be in your way or anything."

"Oh, we can hide *everything*," Stanley said. "We'll put the wires under the rugs, and put the speakers in the cupboards, and you just won't know that there's anything there."

"Hmph," Mrs. Pearson said. "I'll believe *that* when I see it, Stanley Pearson. Every project you boys start always messes up the house in some way or other, and I don't suppose electronics will be any different from the others. Come along, Jenny, it's time for you to go to bed."

Jenny stopped at the bottom of the stairs. "Good night, Uncle Harold," she called. "And thanks a lot for my earrings, I'm going to wear them all night."

"Say," Uncle Harold said after she had disappeared upstairs, "I had no idea those earrings would make such a hit." He looked at his watch. "I'd better get started for Southwick pretty soon, but before I go I want to show you two what to do with this amplifier."

He took a coil of wire out of the carton and put it on the table. The boys drew up chairs and they put their three heads together over the amplifier. When Mrs. Pearson came back into the room, she watched them without saying anything.

"All right," Uncle Harold said finally. "You'll probably have that working by breakfast time. But just remember one thing. Don't turn your volume up too loud early in the morning, or your folks aren't going to be very enthusiastic about any more equipment. OK? Now I've got to get back to Southwick."

He thumped Joe and Stanley on their backs and walked over to the door. "Thanks a lot for the supper, Sis. I sure do enjoy eating with the family every now and then. I'll be up again early next week, I think. And I'll bring up some more junk for your young electricians. G'by, Ed." He turned up his coat collar and went out. They could hear the motor starting and warming up, and then the headlights came on and flashed past the windows as the pickup truck turned and went down the driveway.

CHAPTER FOUR

". . . WITH TWENTY PER CENT MORE HORSE-POWER THAN ANY . . ." a deep voice boomed through the house.

Mr. and Mrs. Pearson sat up in bed suddenly.

"What was *that?*" they both said at once.

Mr. Pearson pushed one leg out from under the covers, and then stopped. "Oh, I know. The amplifier. I guess the boys got it hooked up all right. And only five after *six!* I suppose they woke up Jenny with all that racket." He stuck his leg back under the bedclothes again and pulled the covers over his head. "That's the end of peace and quiet around this house," he muttered from under the blanket.

Up in Joe's room it was quiet again, but not peaceful. Joe was scowling at his brother.

"I *told* you not to fiddle with that volume control," he hissed. "Now we'll have Mom and Pop on our necks any minute. And you've probably woken up Jenny, so we won't be able to play that trick on her."

"But I didn't *know* it was the volume," Stanley whispered back. "I thought it was the other one, the one that makes it deep or squeaky."

"Oh, sure," Joe said. "And it just has VOLUME in big letters right over it. Now keep quiet. I'm going to listen out in the hall."

He pushed the door open slowly and stuck his head out. Nothing was stirring. The only sound was the ticking of the grandfather clock at the bottom of the stairs.

"OK, Stanley," he whispered. "I'll take the speaker down the hall, and you pay out the wire behind me. And don't make any noise." He held the speaker in both hands and crept along the passage, keeping near the wall where the boards didn't squeak so much. Stanley carefully payed out the wire hand over hand, taking care that it didn't drag on the floor. When Joe reached Jenny's door, he put the speaker down in the corner and pointed it straight at the door. Then he tiptoed back to his own room.

"There," Joe said. "Now we're all set. All we've got to do is wait till she opens her door. I'll keep watch, and when I raise my hand, you turn it up to full volume."

"But what about Mom and Pop?" Stanley wondered. "I don't think they're going to like it if they get woken up."

"Well, it's almost quarter to seven, and they get up then. If Jenny only stays asleep until they're up, everything will be OK."

In a few minutes they heard their mother going down the stairs to the kitchen, and then they heard the water splashing in the bathroom. That meant that their father had started shaving.

"Good," Joe said. "Now Jenny can wake up any time she wants. Put on your earphones, Stanley, so you can tell what's going on. But keep your hand on the volume button so you'll be ready."

Stanley slipped on the earphones and listened for a moment, his eyes squinting up at the ceiling. "Mush," he said. "A girl's singing about how somebody doesn't love her any more, or something."

"Well, keep me informed," Joe said. "And watch my hand."

Stanley listened, his face twisting into various expressions of discomfort. "Now it's Bromo-Seltzer," he announced.

Joe peered through the crack of his door. No

sound from Jenny yet. "Now it's frozen pies," Stanley reported.

"Now it's news," Stanley said. "All about three men who robbed a bank. And a fire in—"

"*Psst!*" Joe whispered. "I hear her. Get ready."

Jenny's door opened. Joe raised his arm, and Stanley twirled the volume knob. A shattering roar filled the house.

". . . NEAR THE TOWN OF SMACKOVER, ARKANSAS, BUT NO ONE WAS INJURED . . ."

Jenny shrieked and darted back into her room, her hands over her ears.

"Cut it!" Joe ordered. The roar ceased.

Everything was very quiet for about fifteen seconds. Then Mr. Pearson came out of the bathroom, drying his face with a towel.

"What are you boys trying to do, anyway?" he said. "Scare us all to death? You gave me such a start I almost cut my ear off with the razor. And what did you do to Jenny? Did you wake her up with that racket?"

"Oh, no," Joe said. "She was awake before that."

"She was just coming out of her room," Stanley said, "and then it suddenly got loud."

Mr. Pearson looked at the loudspeaker beside

Jenny's door. "I see," he said. "It just suddenly got loud, did it? A strange coincidence, wasn't it? I can see we're going to have to establish some house rules about the use of amplifiers after this. You'd better get dressed now, and we'll have a public hearing at breakfast."

At breakfast Mrs. Pearson was patient, but very firm. "I can put up with wires and megaphones around the house," she said, "but I simply am *not* going to stand for any more terrible *noise*. Why, we'd all be deaf before the end of the week. You almost scared Jenny out of a year's growth. Her ears are more sensitive than yours, and a noise like that could hurt her. You two can practice with these radio things all you want, but you'll have to do it *quietly*."

"OK, Mom," Joe said. "We were just experimenting this morning. We'll try not to let it happen again."

"I suggest you try hard," Mr. Pearson said. "Because if it *did* happen again, we might have to give the amplifier back to Uncle Harold."

"Oh, no," Joe said. "We wouldn't want that to happen. We'll be awfully quiet from now on. Won't we, Stanley?"

"Sure," Stanley said. "Like mice."

Joe, Stanley and Jenny were climbing the hill on the way home from school that afternoon, when a big Coca-Cola truck pulled up beside them. The driver leaned across the seat and called to them.

"Hey, Bud, this where the Pearsons live?"

Joe nodded. "Right in that house there."

"Well, I got a box of things from Harold Watts down in Southwick. He asked me to drop it off at the Pearsons' on my way through. It's full of wires, it looks like."

"That's from our Uncle Harold," Joe said. "You can give us the box here if you want, and we'll carry it up to the house."

"It's pretty heavy," the driver said. "You better hop in and I'll drive you up there."

They all squeezed into the cab, and the truck went up to the top of the hill and stopped at their mailbox that had *E. PEARSON* painted on the side. The driver got out and swung a big carton down from the truck. He looked into the box. "What you gonna do with all this stuff, sonny? You starting a new telephone company or something?"

"No," Joe said. "Not yet anyway. We're just learning about electronics."

The driver climbed back into his cab. "Well, take it easy, Mac," he said. "That stuff looks dangerous."

"We will," Joe assured him. "And thanks for bringing it."

They watched while the truck drove over the hill, and then the two boys leaned over to pick up the box. "Hey, it *is* heavy," Joe said. "Here, Jenny, take my books, will you?"

Jenny went ahead to open the door while Joe and Stanley staggered up the walk with the box between them. They set it down on the living room floor and started pulling things out of it.

Stanley put his head inside. "Hey, it's *full* of speakers and microphones and stuff. And here's a kind of switchboard thing."

"Let's see," Joe said. "Say, now we can set up the intercom. This is just what we need. And here's lots of wire. Coils and coils of it."

Jenny came back from the kitchen nibbling a cookie. She handed one each to her brothers, who ate them absent-mindedly, still pulling objects out of the box with their free hands.

"You see, this will be easy," Joe said. "All we've gotta do is plug these microphone wires into the amplifier, and then put the microphones around the house, and hook on the switchboard, and we're all set to listen in anywhere in the place."

"Well, c'mon," Stanley said. "Let's start putting

them up. This is going to be *neat*. Maybe we can get it working by suppertime."

The boys picked up two of the microphones, and began uncoiling wires all the way up the stairs and into Joe's room. Stanley came downstairs again and hung a microphone over the portrait of Great-aunt Hannah, and then he ran upstairs. There was a heated discussion about which wire went where, because the connections on the switchboard were pretty complicated.

Jenny was still sitting on the sofa chewing the last piece of her second cookie and looking at the portrait. Great-aunt Hannah looked funny with a round black microphone hanging over her left eye.

"Jenny!" Joe called from upstairs. "Say something into that microphone, will you? We want to see if it works."

Jenny got up and walked over to Aunt Hannah's picture. "Hello," she said. "Hello hello hello hello." She walked to the door and called upstairs. "Did you hear that?"

"No!" Joe called back. "Just a minute. We've got to make some adjustments." Jenny could hear them arguing about the wires once more.

"OK," Joe called then. "Try it again, Jenny."

Jenny faced the portrait as before. "Hello, Aunt

Hannah," she said. "How do you like that thing hanging over your eye? Does it—"

"It works!" the boys shouted. "It works fine! Now try talking softly and we'll turn the volume way up and see if we can catch it."

"Can you hear this, you sillies?" Jenny said in a very low voice.

"It's *wonderful!*" the boys shouted. Stanley dashed down the stairs to try the microphone himself. "This is *great!*" he said. "People are going to have to be awful careful what they say around here after this. We can hear *everything!*"

"Hey, Stanley," Joe called down to him. "Bring up another microphone and a speaker, and we'll rig up an intercom to the kitchen so Mom can call us to supper over it."

By suppertime the boys had established contact with the kitchen, with a microphone and speaker standing on the shelf next to the kitchen clock, and Mrs. Pearson had been given detailed instructions about their use. When supper was ready, she leaned over to the microphone and shrieked, "Kitchen to control room!"

"Ouch, Ma!" Joe's voice came from the speaker. "You don't have to shout like that. We've got the volume turned up, so you can just talk, right from the middle of the room, or wherever you are. Try it again, will you, Ma?"

"Well, all right, but I've got some biscuits in the oven and I'll have to hurry. Kitchen to control room?"

"Control room to kitchen," the speaker said. "What is it? Over."

"Supper's ready. Don't forget to wash up. Over."

"Roger, Ma. We'll be right down."

Within two minutes Joe and Stanley were sitting at the table, their hands and faces still damp from the washing.

"My goodness," Mrs. Pearson said. "You boys have never come to meals so quick in your whole lives."

"That's the beauty of an intercom, you see?" Stanley said, wiping his neck with his sleeve. "It gets instant action. There's really nothing like it."

CHAPTER FIVE

BY THE END of November the Pearson house was pretty well wired. Every few days another box of equipment would come from Uncle Harold, and Joe and Stanley were scarcely able to keep up with the growing collection of speakers and microphones and telephones and switchboards. For a month now they had been having music during supper, for the boys had set up a record player in Joe's room, and they could turn it off and on from the supper table. They had only one record—a long-playing recording of the *Grand Canyon Suite* that Uncle Harold had found in a secondhand portable phonograph—but they played it every night for a month, until Mr. Pearson started to roll his eyes whenever he heard "Sunrise over the Canyon" beginning.

By flipping the proper switches, Joe and Stanley

could listen to the same music in the kitchen when it was their turn to do dishes, or out in the back yard if they were raking leaves. The outside loud-speaker was a powerful one, and it could be heard all the way down to Stony Brook, at the bottom of the hill. Or if they wanted to hear the Saturday football games over the radio, all they had to do was turn a dial on the switchboard in Joe's room, and they could listen to the game anywhere they wanted.

Joe's room was the main control room for the system and it looked it. One half of the room was filled up with amplifiers, switchboards, the record player and a whole battery of microphones and speakers for the intercom system, and there were so many wires leading in and out of the door and window that Uncle Harold had said it looked like a halfway house on the Atlantic Cable.

There were microphones and speakers in every room now, and they all could talk back and forth from room to room without even raising their voices. Nobody had to shout any more. As a matter of fact, everyone began to talk in lower and lower tones, because you could never tell when your microphone was turned on or not, and you never could be sure that what you were saying wasn't going to be broadcast in another room upstairs, or perhaps boomed at full volume to all outdoors.

And then things got more complicated when the tape recorder came. It was a small one that Uncle Harold had picked up on a trade-in, but Mrs. Pearson had objected to such a valuable gift.

"I just don't think it's right for those boys to have such expensive things," she said. "You're giving them too much, Harold."

But Uncle Harold told her not to worry. "You see," he said, "people trade in these small sets and buy bigger ones or better ones, and the manufacturers don't like us to sell them again. They want us to keep them off the market so they can sell new ones. So I've got eight used tape recorders on my shelves right now, and I can't use more than one at a time myself. Might as well have somebody enjoy them. I'd like to send up a couple more if Joe and Stanley can think of some way to use them."

"Oh, sure, Uncle Harold," Joe said. "We can think of lots of ways to use them."

And they did, too. At first the boys connected up the tape recorder to the intercom, and recorded various things that were being said around the house during the day, and then played them back after supper each evening. It was a lot of fun. There was a recording of Stanley singing in the shower, which Mr. Pearson said sounded like the sinking of the *Titanic,* and there was a recording of Mrs. Pearson scolding the whole household for tracking mud across the rug—that number went on for exactly six minutes without a pause and was one of the favorites for everybody except Mrs. Pearson. There was a recording of Joe practicing a two-minute speech for English class entitled "My Trip to Northampton, Mass." with long *errr's* while the speaker tried to find where he was in his notes. There was a very soft-voiced recording of Jenny telling a story to Mrs. Lumpkin, an elderly, one-legged rag doll. It was a nice story, but it always upset Jenny dreadfully whenever she heard it because it was meant to be a private story, so there was a rule that it could be played only when Jenny was in bed. The best recording of all, the boys thought, was the one they made when their father knocked the full can of paint off the stepladder. It was a good loud one, with lots of lively words in it, but they'd heard it only once, because Mr. Pearson had ordered it erased. There was a big argument about that, because there had been an understanding that nobody could erase anything without unanimous consent of the family. Mr. Pearson finally won his wife over to his side,

and then there were threats of sanctions and the recording was officially banned. It was too bad, because it was the best one they ever made.

Then when Uncle Harold brought up the other tape recorders, they had an even better idea. They set up three recorders in a row on the shelf in Joe's room. Each one had a different recording all ready to play. They were all in Mrs. Pearson's voice, one calling the children in from outdoors in that long, high-pitched call that carried so far across the fields, another announcing in a businesslike voice that it was time to wash up for supper, and the third calling each of the family by name and asking if they were out of bed yet, because it was almost time for breakfast. Each machine was connected to a small switchboard in the kitchen, and all Mrs. Pearson had to do was to push the right button and the tape recorder would go into action. There were a few mixups at first, and once or twice Mrs. Pearson hit the wrong button, and her voice went echoing out over the hillside calling them in from outdoors when the family were all still in bed in the morning, or telling them to get up for breakfast when it was really time to wash up for supper.

Later, when the boys had the time-switch rigged up, they had it arranged so their mother's voice came on automatically at five minutes of seven every morning without her having to do anything about it. They had a little trouble sometimes because they kept forgetting to switch it off for Sunday mornings, and then there was the time that Teddy Watson had been fooling around with the controls and the voice began calling out at half past two in the morning.

"Time to get up!" it called out cheerfully in the darkness. "Come on, all you lazybones, wake up! Ed Pearson, are you awake? Are you getting out of bed? Now don't roll over and go back to sleep. Stanley, are you awake? Come on now, Joe, rise and shine! It's almost time for—" By the time Joe snapped off the switch everybody was nicely awake, and there was a lot of grumbling about the Pearson Brothers' Automatic Morning Call System when breakfast time really did come, about five hours later.

But that wasn't all. The Pearson Brothers' Electronics Enterprises had other plans.

Joe and Stanley put their heads together, and finally decided to build a machine to answer the telephone when nobody was home. When Uncle Harold came up in the middle of December he was impressed with the telephone-answering machine.

"That's mighty ingenious," he said admiringly. "But what do you do if you want to answer the phone yourself? This machinery starts going into action as soon as the bell rings."

"It sure does," Mr. Pearson said. "You have to run to get to the phone before the conversation is all over. The neighbors are getting used to it now, though, and they usually wait a bit before they start talking. Then I always forget to push the shut-off button at the beginning, and that causes a lot of confusion. They don't know whether it's me answering or the tape recorder."

"It makes me *nervous*," Mrs. Pearson said. "I haven't been able to have a nice comfortable chat on the telephone since they rigged this up. I get all mixed up about the buttons, and voices start coming out of all these recording machines, and sometimes I don't know whether I'm talking to *this* person, or the one who called last time, and once I even found I was talking to *myself*, and the other person had hung up a long time before. And my friends don't like it either. The first thing they say is 'Is that you, Vera, or is it that machine I'm talking to?'"

"Oh, they'll probably get used to that pretty soon," Uncle Harold said. "But there's something else that you ought to know about. You see there's a law that says you've got to have a beep tone every fifteen seconds if you're recording a conversation over the telephone. I wouldn't want you kids to get into any trouble with the law with this machine of yours."

Joe and Stanley smiled at each other. "Oh, that's all right, Uncle Harold," Joe said. "We read about that in the phone book, and it's all taken care of."

"Well, how is it taken care of?" Uncle Harold wanted to know.

"It was a cinch," Stanley said. "After Joe made the recording that answers the phone, I just said 'beep' into the dictaphone every fifteen seconds, so when it answers the phone, the beep tone keeps right on going every fifteen seconds all the time anybody's talking."

But Uncle Harold didn't look quite satisfied. "But I didn't hear any beep tone just now when I listened to it. How come?"

"That's simple," Joe said. "You only have to have a beep tone every fifteen seconds, and sometimes people don't talk that long. The law doesn't say you got to have a beep tone when you *start* talking."

Uncle Harold couldn't help smiling. "Well, I must say you kids have figured all the angles. I got to hand it to you."

Uncle Harold was rather thoughtful during supper, but right in the middle of dessert he said, "You know, you two boys have a real knack for this electrical stuff. I think you're about ready to branch out on something new. What do you think?"

"Sure thing," Joe and Stanley both said.

"Well," Uncle Harold went on, "I've just got hold of something in my shop—I'm not going to tell what it is, so don't ask—a department store in Westfield turned it in for a bigger model, and I thought maybe I might send it up here for a special Christmas present. Oh, yes, and I'll send up a present for Jenny too."

"Can't you spend Christmas with us, Uncle Harold?" Jenny asked.

"I'd like to, Jenny, but I promised I'd visit my cousin George's family over in Agawam for Christmas. But I could come up for New Year's, and maybe we could have a big sliding party on your hill if we get some snow. What do you think?"

"That's a fine idea, Harold," Mrs. Pearson said. "We could invite the school children and the teachers, too, and have cocoa and cookies."

"And a bonfire at the top of the hill to keep everybody warm," Mr. Pearson said. "Much more fun with a bonfire."

Joe looked doubtful. "Do you think we ought to have the teachers too? Miss McCallum's pretty old for sliding, don't you think? She must be about eighty years old, and kind of brittle, I shouldn't wonder, and we wouldn't want her to fall off and break her neck or anything—I mean not right here on our hill. It would interrupt the sliding and everything."

Stanley's eyes lit up with a happy gleam. "I'd like to see Miss Griffin on a sled. I'd point her right toward the Six Bumps and see what happened. Maybe she wouldn't sit up so straight after that."

"Stanley!" Mrs. Pearson said. "You know Miss Griffin is a very nice lady, even though she is a little strict at times."

"Oh, sure," Stanley said. "But it would be fun just the same."

"Miss Romaine's not old," Jenny said. "She *likes* sliding. She's only been a teacher for two years, and she's *very* nice."

"She is nice," Mrs. Pearson agreed, "and pretty, too. And I think we should invite Miss McCallum and Miss Griffin to come along too, and if they would rather not go sliding, they can stand by the bonfire and keep warm."

"I'm going to be very generous and lend Miss Griffin my sled," Stanley said. "And I'll tie the handles down so she can't steer."

"Well, I can see it's going to be quite a party," Uncle Harold said. "I've got to run along now, but I'll send up those presents, and I'll be seeing you at New Year's."

CHAPTER SIX

TWO DAYS before Christmas Mr. Hagerty's truck drove into the Pearsons' back yard. (Mr. Hagerty ran the garage in Pearson's Corners, and he did some trucking in his spare time.) Joe and Stanley ran out. It was cold, and the wind was rippling the canvas on the top of the truck.

Mr. Hagerty got out of the cab and pulled up his sheepskin collar. "Hello there, boys," he called. "Your Uncle Harold asked me to leave off some boxes for you. They're not supposed to be opened till Christmas. He wanted me to tell you that. And he said for heaven's sake don't drop them."

He went around to the rear of the truck and pulled out a big square carton that had FRAGILE on it in big red letters. He rested it on the tailgate, and then pulled out another smaller carton. "You boys take this one," he said. "But take it easy. I promised your uncle I'd get them into the house without breaking anything." Mr. Hagerty hoisted the big carton up on his shoulder, and Joe and Stanley carried the small carton between them. It was very heavy for its size, they noticed. They put the boxes in a corner of the living room, behind the big chair.

Mr. Hagerty stopped in the kitchen to speak to Mrs. Pearson. "I understand you're having the school kids out here for New Year's," he said. "That'll be a nice treat. My little girl's been talking about it for a week. They sure do like sliding on the big hill."

"I just hope we get some snow before then," Mrs. Pearson said. "It won't be much fun without that."

"Oh, we'll get snow, I guess. The radio said snow for tomorrow. I've got to get down to the garage and hitch on the snowplow. Have a Merry Christmas."

He went out and shut the door, but in a minute he was back again. "I almost forgot," he said. "Harold sent this along, too. It's a present for Jenny, he said. I had it on the seat in the cab."

It was a smallish package done up in brown paper and string. Stanley put it behind the chair in the living room with the other boxes.

"Where *is* Jenny?" he asked when he came back.

"Upstairs, playing with her dollhouse, I think," Mrs. Pearson said.

"Jenny's awful quiet these days, isn't she?" Joe said. "She used to rip around a lot more than she does now. Maybe she's sick or something."

Stanley pulled a long face. "Jeepers, I hope not. It'd be terrible to have her sick over Christmas. We'd all have to keep quiet and go tiptoeing around just when we wanted to make a big racket."

"There's nothing wrong about being quiet," his mother told him. "You may not believe it, but some people actually *like* to be quiet now and then. And there hasn't been much quiet around this house since you boys began fooling around with those megaphones and things."

"Not megaphones, Mom," Stanley said. "They're *microphones.*"

The next morning it was snowing hard. Snowflakes were blowing against the windowpanes, and outdoors everything was white everywhere you looked. Joe and Stanley were out shoveling the front walk when Mr. Hagerty's truck came by with the big yellow plow on the front. Mr. Hagerty couldn't stop, but he waved, and the plow piled up a mountain of snow at the end of the front walk.

In the afternon the three children went down the hill and across Stony Brook to the woods beyond and cut down a good-sized Christmas tree.

"It's kind of thin on one side," Jenny said, looking down at the tree lying in the snow.

"There's some lots better ones beyond the stone wall," Stanley suggested. "Why don't we cut one of those?"

Joe shook his head. "We can't do that. Mr. Watson only lets us cut trees on this side of the wall. And Pop says we better do what Mr. Watson says, or he might not let us cut trees at all."

"This all Mr. Watson's land?" Stanley wondered.

"Sure," Joe said. "The whole thing. From our house all the way to the Watsons'."

"And the big hill?"

"Sure."

"And Stony Brook too?" Jenny asked.

"Yup," Joe said. He stuck his ax handle under a branch of the Christmas tree. "C'mon, Stanley, grab hold of the handle and we'll drag this home. If you follow behind us, Jenny, you can walk in our tracks."

"How come he owns so much?" Stanley wondered.

"Well, he probably bought it, or somebody did.

49

Anyway, it's his, and he can do whatever he wants with it, I guess."

Jenny was plodding along behind the tree, thinking. "I hope Mr. Watson doesn't do anything to Stony Brook," she said. "That's my favorite place, and I wouldn't want it to be changed. At all."

When Mr. Pearson got home that afternoon they nailed the tree on its stand and then decorated it. Joe fixed up the lights and hooked up a recording of "Hark the Herald Angels Sing" that he had taken from a radio program. He fixed it so that when the tree lights were turned on the music began to play, and then to make it even more automatic, he attached it to a door switch, so whenever anyone opened the door to the living room, the lights would go on and the music would start playing. He wanted to put in a blinker button, so the tree lights would flash on and off, but Mrs. Pearson drew the line at that.

Christmas morning is not a good time for sleeping, and by the time the Pearson Brothers' Automatic Morning Call went on, the family had already finished breakfast and were gathered around the tree to open presents. Since Uncle Harold's presents were the biggest and most exciting looking of all,

the family agreed to open them last. After all the useful family presents were opened—a pair of slippers for Joe, and a dress for Jenny, and wool socks for Stanley—Jenny unwrapped her package from Uncle Harold and found a little box with two dials on it. There was a note from Uncle Harold that said:

DEAR JENNY:
This is a transistor radio. I noticed that you didn't have a radio in your dollhouse, and maybe you can use this. It runs on a couple of flashlight batteries and they should last a long time. Hope the dolls like it.

Uncle Harold's present to the boys was the big event. Stanley had been making all kinds of guesses, like a burglar alarm, or a mechanical bed-making machine, or a jukebox, but Joe just shook his head. They cut open the carton at one side and pulled out a black metal cabinet. It had a glass screen on one side.

"It's a TV set!" Stanley shouted. "Whoopee! That was the one thing we needed. Now we've got *everything*."

"But what's in the other box?" Joe wondered. "Stop jumping around, Stanley, and give me the knife so I can open this one."

In the smaller carton was a heavy black machine with a big lens on one end.

"What is it?" Stanley asked.

"Don't know," Joe said. "Wait, here's a note from Uncle Harold.

"DEAR JOE AND STANLEY:

What you see in these two boxes is a closed-circuit television system. That means it has its own camera which broadcasts to its own TV screen, so you can set up the camera in one room and watch what goes on there on the TV set in another room. I've marked the cables, so you"ll know how to hook them up. A store in Westfield had used this set, and they traded it in for a bigger one with more cameras. Merry Christmas! from UNCLE HAROLD."

"Wow!" Stanley shouted. "It's a real TV set! And a TV camera too! Jeepers, it looks just about brand-new. That Westfield store must have been awful careful with it. No scratches or anything."

Mr. Pearson came over and looked closely. "You mean this can take pictures in one place and receive them in another? Just like a TV broadcasting station?"

"Sure," Joe said. "Except this broadcasting station has its own private little channel, and other people can't get it on their sets. That's what a closed-circuit TV system is."

"But what did the Westfield store want with it?" Mrs. Pearson wanted to know. "How could they use it?"

"Oh, lots of stores have them now," Joe said. "They hide the camera in the wall somewhere, and the manager can sit in his office watching the TV screen, and see whether the customers are snitching any of the merchandise. He could watch the sales-girls too, to see if they're keeping on the job. It's quite an invention."

"It sounds kind of sneaky to me," Jenny said. "I wouldn't like to have any old TV watching me all the time."

"Well," Stanley said, "let's not just sit around and *talk* about it. We got to get this thing set up some-where. Where'll we put it first?"

"Set up your camera in the kitchen," Mr. Pear-son said. "Then your mother can sit in the living room and see who's swiping cookies out of the cookie jar."

Joe and Stanley didn't think much of that idea. "I've got a better plan," Joe said. "Set it up in the bathroom and we can tell whether Stanley brushes his teeth or not."

"Hah!" Stanley said. "We ought to set it up in Joe's room, and then we can see whether he's doing his homework or reading a comic book."

"You and me'd better work *together* on this," Joe said quickly. "We'll start the Pearson Brothers' Investigation Service, and we'll set up wherever we're needed. And we'll agree not to investigate each other, OK?"

"OK," Stanley said. "Now let's take the stuff upstairs."

With a great deal of heaving and pushing, the boys got the television equipment up the stairs and into Joe's room, which now was so crowded that there was only a narrow passage leading from the door to the bed. The rest of the day the two boys spent upstairs, running wires here and there, carrying soldering irons and screwdrivers from one room to another, and talking in low earnest voices. By suppertime they had the television screen set up in Joe's room, on top of the bureau because there was no other place for it. The TV camera had disappeared somewhere, and Joe and Stanley weren't saying where it was.

That night when Mrs. Pearson came upstairs to tuck Jenny in, Jenny was sitting on her bed, with her knees tucked up under her chin and her toes sticking out from under her blue nightgown.

"Well, Jenny," Mrs. Pearson said, "was it a nice Christmas?"

"Yes, Mommy."

"Wasn't it nice of Uncle Harold to give you that tiny little radio?"

"Mmmm."

Mrs. Pearson looked at her. "You don't sound very enthusiastic, Jenny. Don't you like it?"

Jenny shook her head slowly. "I put it in my dollhouse, just so Uncle Harold won't feel bad about it, but I'm not ever going to turn it on. You know, Mommy, there are just *too many* machines talking and listening all over our house. Everything gets so noisy, and all those voices keep shouting out all the time and I don't know which are real voices and which are electrical ones, and I get all tangled up and it makes my ears ring inside. And I don't like people listening to me when they're not here. So in my dollhouse no one's ever going to do anything like that. But don't tell Uncle Harold, will you, Mommy?"

"No, Jenny, I won't tell him. Now crawl under the covers and don't worry about the voices any more. Those boys will get tired of all their electrical equipment after a while, and then everything will be peaceful again. Now, good night."

"Good night, Mommy."

Mrs. Pearson closed the door softly and went downstairs. She sat down on the couch with Mr. Pearson and heaved a relaxing sigh. It had been a long day.

"What's the matter with the Christmas tree lights?" she wondered. "They were working all right before supper."

"Oh, the boys took that door switch. They needed it for something they were doing upstairs."

"Where *are* the boys, anyway? They're being awfully quiet."

There was a low buzzing in the corner of the living room, which warned them that the loud-speaker had been turned on.

"Attention, please," a voice said. "This is the Pearson Brothers' Investigating Service reporting on Case Number One. Our special equipment shows that Miss Jenny Pearson is sucking a candy cane. She got up and got it off her table. That is all."

Immediately there was a loud wail from Jenny's room, and Mr. and Mrs. Pearson had to go upstairs to quiet things down.

Jenny was climbing into bed again, and she was in tears. "Joe and Stanley must of been peeking at me, and that isn't fair! It isn't any of their business if I want to get up and get something. I don't like to have them spying on me! It's awful!"

"There, there, Jenny," her mother said. "No harm's done, and we'll go speak to the boys about it. Now you go to sleep and forget all about it."

They looked into Joe's room and found the boys sitting innocently on the bed.

"Jenny says you boys have been peeking at her," Mr. Pearson said. "Is that right?"

"We haven't been out of this room since Jenny came up to bed," Joe said.

Stanley grinned happily. "We've just been sitting right here the whole time."

"Well, how did you know that Jenny had gotten up to get the candy cane?"

"Oh, we've got her under investigation," Joe said. "But we're the modern kind of detectives. We don't go around peeking in keyholes. We just sit here and watch our TV screen."

"We rigged up the camera on her closet shelf," Stanley said cheerfully. "And then we plugged in an extension on her lamp cord, so when she turned on her light a warning light would go on in our room, and we could watch our screen. It worked perfectly. We saw her walk to the table and pick up the candy cane and then climb back into bed. It was neat."

"Jenny didn't think so," Mrs. Pearson said. "She was very upset. You'll have to stop this peeking and prying."

"It wouldn't bother her if she wasn't doing anything wrong," Joe said. "She's just got a guilty conscience, that's all."

"Maybe you boys would have a guilty conscience if someone was watching *you* on a TV screen," Mr. Pearson said. "You're a fine pair to be snooping around checking up on people. How did you happen to get elected to that job, I wonder?"

"Well, we're the ones who have the TV set," Joe said. "I guess the way it works is that the guys with the equipment are the ones who do the snooping."

CHAPTER SEVEN

THE MORNING of the sliding party was bright and clear. The sun was sparkling on the new snow and everybody was in high spirits. That is, everybody but Jenny. She didn't come down to breakfast.

"I looked at her over the TV," Joe reported. "And she didn't look so good. She was all curled up in bed with her arm over her head."

Mrs. Pearson pushed the intercom button. "Hello, Jenny? How do you feel?"

"No good. My ear hurts."

"Oh, beans," Stanley said. "She *would* come down with something right on the day of the sliding party."

"And I'm going to be *so* busy today," Mrs. Pearson said. "I've got all those cookies to bake, and the sandwiches, and the cocoa. I don't know *when* I'll find time to take care of Jenny. And ears can cause real trouble, too. I'll have to call Dr. Pratt right after breakfast."

"I got an idea, Ma," Joe said. "I'll bring down the TV set, and you can keep an eye on Jenny right here in the kitchen."

"Well, perhaps that would be a good plan," she said. "That would save me running up and down stairs all day."

"That would be a big help, Joe," Mr. Pearson said. "And after you do that, you and Stanley ought to get that bonfire ready for this evening. You'll find some old boards out in back of the tool shed, and Gus Thornburg said he would give us a lot of scraps from his carpenter shop. Hagerty's going to bring them up on his truck sometime this morning."

"OK, Pop," Joe said. "We'll build up a big old pile, and have it all ready to touch off as soon as it gets dark."

Mrs. Pearson put a little warm oil in Jenny's ear, but it was still hurting by mid-morning. Dr. Pratt came and sat on the edge of the bed and took Jenny's temperature.

"Temperature's normal," Dr. Pratt said. "Which ear hurts, Jenny?"

"This one," Jenny said, pointing to her left ear.

Dr. Pratt got out a little instrument with a light in it and peered into her ear. "Can't *see* any trouble," he said. "What does it feel like?"

"It kind of aches," Jenny said. "And there's a buzzing noise sometimes. Almost like someone talking."

"You're hearing things, eh?" Dr. Pratt said. "Do noises seem unusually loud to you? This, for instance?" He snapped his fingers near Jenny's head.

"Ouch!" Jenny said. "It's so loud it hurts."

"That's curious," Dr. Pratt said. "Have you had some loud noises near your ear lately?"

"The boys tried to frighten her with a loudspeaker turned on full blast," Mrs. Pearson said. "But that was back in November."

"Hum," the doctor said. "Somehow your ear has become oversensitive to sounds, Jenny. Sometimes a very loud noise can disturb the small bones in the ear—the ones they call the hammer and stirrup. I knew of a man who worked at a drop forge, and he claimed his ears got so sensitive that he could hear his radio even when it was turned off. Nobody believed his other stories either. But you don't look very sick, Jenny, and I think you'll be all right again soon. Take one of these pills after every meal, and we'll see how things are tomorrow." He closed up his black satchel and tweaked Jenny's toes under the bedclothes. "Probably a little too much Christmas, that's all. You just take it easy today, and stay in bed and keep warm."

"Will I have to miss the sliding party?"

"I'm afraid so," Dr. Pratt said.

A small tear started down Jenny's cheek, but she wiped it off with the edge of the sheet. "Well, maybe Miss Romaine can come up here and say hello to me. Do you think she could, Mommy?"

Mrs. Pearson nodded. "I think she could, Jenny."

When Dr. Pratt had gone, Mrs. Pearson went back to the kitchen and began making peanut butter and jelly sandwiches as fast as she could. Already there was a great pile of oatmeal cookies on the kitchen table, and the cocoa was beginning to warm up in the big aluminum kettle. Every now and then she would look over at the TV screen on the counter. The screen showed Jenny sleeping, with one arm around the one-legged Mrs. Lumpkin. Outside, Joe and Stanley were piling up wood for the bonfire. Mr. Hagerty had dumped a truckload of scrap lumber in the back yard, and the boys were carting it on their sleds to the crest of the hill.

Uncle Harold drove in with his pickup truck, and ran an extension cord from the back porch to the corner of the tool shed, where he nailed up a big floodlight.

By the middle of the afternoon the school children began to arrive, climbing up the road from the village with their sleds trailing along behind them. It was a cold, crisp afternoon, and the sun went down and left the sky pink overhead and green all around the edge, and the snow was just perfect for sliding, with a good crust underneath and a little soft snow on top, so you could go anywhere without sinking in, and all down the long hill people were steering their sleds this way and that, or walking slowly up the hill again.

When it got darker the stars came out and Mr. Pearson lit the bonfire and it blazed way up in big orange flames, and the sparks floated up into the sky.

Stanley offered Miss Griffin his sled, and she said how nice, and then she and Miss McCallum sat on it. That left him without a sled and he had to ride double with Andy Zwillinger the rest of the afternoon.

But Miss Romaine loved the sliding. She was using Jenny's sled, and she even went down over the Six Bumps on a dare. She had on red earmuffs, and her black hair was flying and everybody watched her all the way down to see if she would fall off, but she didn't. And Uncle Harold was having the time of his life. He organized a game of follow-the-leader on sleds, and then he did some stunts and got everybody laughing. He took one trip standing up on the sled and almost made it to the bottom. He left quite a dent in the snow where he landed. He got so much snow down inside his collar that he had to go into the kitchen and dry off.

Mrs. Pearson was heating a second kettleful of cocoa. "Mr. Peterson gave us twelve extra quarts of milk for the party," she said, "and I've got to use it up, if only the cocoa powder will hold out. How did you get so wet, Harold?"

"Oh, I took a header into the snow. I tried to go down standing up. Almost made it too."

"You still like to show off, don't you, Harold? You'll break your neck one of these days."

Uncle Harold pulled out his shirt tails and held them out over the stove to dry. "Say, that Miss Romaine is a mighty cute little trick, isn't she?"

"Why, yes," Mrs. Pearson said, looking down into the cocoa kettle. "The children are all very fond of her."

"I should think they would be," Uncle Harold

said. "She looks like an awfully good sport. Why, she's having as much fun as the kids are. And those pink cheeks and snappy eyes—I never had a teacher like that when I was in school."

"I'll bet you never noticed what kind of teacher you had, Harold. You were too busy with your clock springs and things."

"Why, I noticed every one of my teachers. I kept one eye on them all the time. I had to." He tucked his shirt tails in again and put on his jacket and his mittens.

Mrs. Pearson poured some steaming cocoa into a big metal pitcher. "Take this cocoa out with you, Harold, will you? And tell Ed to bring back the other pitcher when he has a chance. You'd better take two hands to it. I'll open the door for you."

But just at that moment the door opened, and Miss Romaine came in.

"Oh, good evening, Mrs. Pearson," she said. "I just came in to say hello to Jenny. Do you think she's asleep?"

Mrs. Pearson glanced over at the television screen. "No. She's not asleep, I guess. She's looking out the window. By the way, Miss Romaine, I'd like you to meet my brother, Harold Watts. You probably saw him out on the hill."

Miss Romaine smiled a little stiffly. "Indeed I did. So you're the Uncle Harold that Jenny keeps talking about. She's told me a great deal about you."

"Oh, she has?" Uncle Harold said, a little nervously. The cocoa pitcher was beginning to feel hot through his mittens. "Well, I hope she hasn't told too much."

"Why, not at all," Miss Romaine said. "She told me how you do all these *cute little tricks* with electric wire. Of course Jenny is a *cute little trick* herself, don't you think, Mr. Watts?"

"Yes . . . yes, she is," Uncle Harold said through the steam from the cocoa.

"In fact," Miss Romaine went on, not talking to anybody in particular, "there are lots of cute little tricks around, from what I hear. But I should think you would turn off the loudspeaker before you start discussing them. It sounds so awfully public when it's broadcast all over the hillside like that. Well, I must run up and see Jenny."

Uncle Harold turned brick red as Miss Romaine left the room, and he almost dropped the cocoa pitcher. He snapped off the microphone switch. "Good grief! Was the kitchen microphone on? Holy cow, Sis, what did I say, anyway?"

"I think you said something about Miss Romaine being a 'cute little trick,' if I recollect."

Uncle Harold groaned. "How did that happen, anyway? Who turned the microphone on in here?"

"You did," Mrs. Pearson said. "You turned it on when you wanted to announce that it was time to eat. Don't you remember?"

"Yes, I guess I did. Was that ever a bright stunt. I'd better get out of here before she comes down again. See you later."

Mrs. Pearson opened the door for him and he went out with the cocoa pitcher trailing a plume of steam.

Jenny was sitting in her window seat wrapped in a blanket. Her room was on a corner of the house, and she could just see the bonfire if she pressed her face against the windowpane. She had been sitting there ever since the bonfire was lit, and she could see the dark silhouettes of people passing in front of the flames. Uncle Harold's floodlight was shining down the hill, and it made great long shadows when anyone walked up the slope.

There was a gentle knock on the door.

"Come in," Jenny said.

Miss Romaine stepped into the room and closed

the door behind her. "Hello, Jenny. How are you feeling?"

"Pretty good, Miss Romaine. My ear doesn't hurt so much now. Was the sliding good fun?"

"Oh, yes. The snow was just wonderful. It was a shame you had to miss it, but you'll be out soon, and then you can make up for it."

Jenny pushed her nose against the windowpane. Miss Romaine sat down beside her on the window seat.

"Did Uncle Harold do some stunts? Sometimes he does some awfully funny things."

"Yes, Jenny, he did some stunts. He fell on his head once."

"Oh," Jenny said. And then neither of them said anything for a while. They looked out on the snow with the shadows moving on it.

"I don't know," Jenny said suddenly. "Because I don't know what it means."

Miss Romaine looked at her in surprise. "What did you say, Jenny?"

"I said I don't know what that word means."

Miss Romaine was puzzled. "What word, Jenny?"

"That word you said—'extraverk,' or whatever it was."

"Extrovert? But I didn't say that, Jenny."

Jenny looked at her with her eyebrows lifted. "But Miss Romaine, you said you wondered if Uncle Harold was always an 'extraverk.' That was why I said I didn't know."

"But Jenny," Miss Romaine said, "I didn't *say* that. I'm sure I didn't."

Jenny looked up at her for a moment. "Maybe you sort of said it to yourself. Did you do that?"

"Well . . . I might have been thinking of something like that," Miss Romaine said. "Yes, I suppose I was. But I'm *sure* I didn't say it so you could hear it."

"But I *did* hear it," Jenny said. "I heard you wondering if Uncle Harold was always an 'extraverk.' And what is an 'extraverk,' anyway, Miss Romaine?"

"Oh, an *extrovert* is a person who—well, it's the opposite of being shy, Jenny."

"I see," Jenny said. And they both looked out at the bonfire again.

"Oh, no," Jenny said. "Not Uncle Harold."

Miss Romaine looked puzzled again. "No *what*, Jenny?"

"I mean no, he isn't married," Jenny said. "That was what you asked, wasn't it?"

"But I didn't say a word, Jenny. I was just looking out at the fire. I didn't open my mouth."

71

"Maybe you were thinking it then," Jenny suggested. "I guess whenever you start thinking, I can hear you. Like that 'extraverk' thing."

"Oh, *dear*," Miss Romaine said. She began to look a little worried. "You know, Jenny, I really think I ought to be going. Your mother probably is anxious to put you to bed."

"Yes," Jenny said. "She is."

"There now," Miss Romaine said. "I'm sure you'll be feeling better in the morning, after you've had a good sleep. Good night, Jenny."

"Good night, Miss Romaine."

Miss Romaine closed the door softly behind her and hurried down the stairs to the kitchen.

"Mrs. Pearson," she said, "I think Jenny seems a little—well, a little queer. Are you sure she doesn't have a fever or something?"

"She seemed all right when I brought up her supper," Mrs. Pearson said. "Does she complain of a headache?"

"Oh, no, not a headache. It was more the things she was saying. As if she were hearing me talk when I wasn't saying anything."

"Oh, dear me," Mrs. Pearson said. "That sounds as if she might be delirious. I'd better go up and look at her."

Mrs. Pearson opened Jenny's door and looked in. Jenny was still sitting at the window.

"Hello, Mommy," Jenny said without turning around. "You really don't need to, because I'm feeling perfectly all right. Honestly. The earache's all gone and everything."

Her mother stared at her. "Don't need to *what*, Jenny?"

"Call the doctor," Jenny said. "Isn't that what you were going to do?"

"Well, I *was* thinking of that, but how did you know?"

"Because I heard you," Jenny said.

"Well, now how could you have heard me when I didn't say anything?"

Jenny sat down on her bed and tried to explain. "You see, Mommy, I think what's happened is this. For some reason, I suddenly began to hear people *thinking*, and whenever they think something, why, I just hear what they're thinking about."

Mrs. Pearson reached over and put her hand on Jenny's forehead. It didn't seem hot to her. "But Jenny," she said, "you can't hear people's thoughts. It just isn't possible."

"But why not, Mommy? It must be possible, because I'm doing it. For instance, you're thinking right now that I'm a little out of my head because of my earache, and you're hoping that when I wake up in the morning I'll be all right again. Isn't that what you're thinking, Mommy? And you're wondering if you ought to call Dr. Pratt now or wait till morning. Isn't that right?"

"Oh, my goodness," Mrs. Pearson said. "I've never seen anything like *this* before. Are you *sure* you feel all right, Jenny?"

There was a knock on the door. "Come in, Uncle Harold," Jenny called out gaily. Uncle Harold came in and sat down on the end of the bed.

"I don't know what to think of this child," Mrs. Pearson said. "She looks perfectly well, but she keeps saying the strangest things."

"Like what?" Uncle Harold said.

"She didn't seem angry at all when she was with me," Jenny declared.

"What?" Uncle Harold said. "Who didn't seem angry?"

"Miss Romaine," Jenny said. "She didn't seem a bit angry with you. She just wondered if you were an 'extraverk,' and then she—"

"Just a *minute!*" Uncle Harold put up his hand. "Who said anything about Miss Romaine?"

Jenny smiled at him. "Nobody, Uncle Harold. But

that's what you were *thinking* when you came in. You were hoping she wouldn't be mad at you for saying something about her over the loudspeaker, because you like her and you—"

"Hold on!" Uncle Harold said, looking at Jenny and then at Mrs. Pearson. "What's going on here anyway? Have you two been gossiping about that boner I pulled down in the kitchen?"

"No, no, Harold," Mrs. Pearson assured him. "I haven't said a word about it."

"Well then who did? Was it Miss Romaine?"

"Oh, no," Jenny said. "She didn't say a thing about it. What was the boner, Uncle Harold?"

"Oh, nothing," he said. "It was just some silly thing I said about her, and it got broadcast all over the hillside by mistake."

"What did you say about her?" Jenny wanted to know.

"Oh, just . . . well, nothing important—"

"That she was a cute little trick?" Jenny said.

"Oh, I know what you've been doing!" Uncle Harold roared. "You've been listening in on the intercom. No wonder you know so much about what's been going on."

"I haven't either," Jenny said. "It's just that I can hear what you're thinking, that's all."

Uncle Harold grinned at her. "That's a good one, Jenny. You must be feeling better, all right."

But Jenny was serious. "Honestly, Uncle Harold, I really can."

"Go on," he said. "What am I thinking now, for instance?"

"You're thinking that maybe you ought to go out and apologize to Miss Romaine for what you said."

Uncle Harold flushed. "Well, you're just guessing that. I tell you what. I'll think of a number, and you tell me what it is. That'll show you up fast enough."

"All right," Jenny said. "You're thinking of eight."

"You were right that time," Uncle Harold admitted. "That was too easy. Try it again."

"Five thousand two hundred and eighty," Jenny said promptly.

"Right again," Uncle Harold said, looking puzzled. "What color am I thinking of?"

"Black," Jenny said.

"Right." Uncle Harold's eyes opened wider. "Say, you're pretty good at this, Jenny. Now here's one more question. What name am I thinking of?"

Jenny turned her head as if she were listening. She frowned a little. "Romaine," she said finally.

Uncle Harold slapped his leg and laughed. "Aha! I caught you that time, Jenny. You're just guessing, and that time you guessed wrong. I thought I'd catch you on that. You can't fool your Uncle Harold, can you?"

Jenny looked at him calmly. "But Uncle Harold, you were thinking of more than one name at a time. You were sort of thinking a little bit about macaroni, or something like that—"

"Marconi," Uncle Harold said. "He invented the wireless."

"But mostly you were thinking about Romaine. That was why I said that."

"Oh, go on," Uncle Harold said.

"But you were, weren't you? Be fair now," Jenny wiggled her finger at him.

"Well, perhaps I was . . . just a little, in the back of my mind," Uncle Harold admitted. "But for goodness' sake, Jenny, how do you do it? What's the trick, anyway?"

"It's no trick. I just listen, that's all. And then I begin to hear these words, and they're what people are thinking. It's very simple."

Mrs. Pearson was making signals toward the door, and Uncle Harold took the hint. "Well, Jenny, I guess I'd better be going. Good night."

In a few minutes Mrs. Pearson joined him in the kitchen. "Well, what do you think of that, now? What do you suppose has got into the child?"

"I haven't the faintest idea," Uncle Harold said. "She *looks* all right to me."

"But she doesn't sound all right. There's something very queer going on, I should say. Do you suppose she really *can* hear people's thoughts?"

Uncle Harold shook his head. "You've got me. But if she *can,* the Pearsons are in for some strange times."

CHAPTER EIGHT

"WELL, JENNY," Mr. Pearson said at breakfast next morning, "it's nice to see you downstairs again. How do you feel?"

"I feel fine," Jenny said.

"You were asleep when I went up to say good night to you last night," her father said, "but they told me you were having quite a game guessing people's thoughts."

"It wasn't a game," Jenny said. "And I wasn't guessing, I was *hearing* their thoughts."

"Hah!" Stanley scoffed. "Who do you think you're kidding?"

"I'm not kidding. Try me out and then you'll see, smarty."

"I'll try you out," Stanley said cheerfully. "I'm thinking of something now. What is it?"

Jenny looked at him for a moment. "You better

write it down on a piece of paper first. Then I'll tell you what it is."

"OK," Stanley said. He went over to the desk in the corner of the room and scrawled something on a sheet of paper, screwing up his face tightly with the effort. "All right, Jenny," he said. "See if you know what *that* is."

"I *do* know," Jenny said. "You were thinking about strawberry jam."

Stanley's face fell, and Joe picked up the paper and showed it to everyone at the table. It had "strabery jam" written on it.

"Well, what do you know about that!" Mr. Pearson said.

Joe had a more professional interest. "Can you do it every time?" he wanted to know. "I mean, with a lot of people at once?"

"I think so," Jenny said. "For instance, you're thinking about maybe making a thought-recording machine, and Mommy's wondering if she ought to do the wash today, and Daddy's wondering if the oil truck can get up our hill, because there isn't much oil left for the furnace, and Uncle Harold—"

"You can leave me out," Uncle Harold said quickly. "You analyzed me last night."

"All right, I'll skip Uncle Harold, and Stanley is

hoping that he can lick the jam spoon when everybody's finished breakfast. How was that?" she said proudly.

They all looked at her in wonder. "That's really remarkable," Mr. Pearson said. "Just how do you do that, anyway?"

"It's very simple," Jenny explained. "When I listen with my right ear, I can hear people talking and all the ordinary sounds, but when I listen with my left ear, then I can hear the sounds inside people's heads."

"But how can you tell which person you're listening to?" Mrs. Pearson wondered. "I should think it would just be a jumble of noises."

"Well, it's pretty mixed up until I think hard about one person, and then I can hear just his thoughts and not the others."

Joe looked at her with growing respect. "How far away can you reach, Jenny? Do you have to be in the same room, or can you tune in on people farther away?"

"I don't know," Jenny said. "I haven't really tried it out yet."

"Well, let's try it," Joe suggested. "I'll go upstairs and think about something, and you try to hear me." He darted out of the room.

Jenny turned her head and listened. "He might think about making his bed," Mrs. Pearson murmured, but everyone said "Sh!" at her.

"All right," Jenny said. "I've got it."

They called Joe downstairs again. "What was I thinking?" he asked eagerly.

"You thought about only six more days before school begins again."

"That's *right!* Good work, Jenny! Did you get clear reception? Was it weak? Any static?"

"Oh, it was very clear," Jenny said. "I think I could do it much farther away than that."

"Try Teddy Watson," Stanley said. "He's about a quarter of a mile away. See if you can get him."

"I'll try," Jenny said. She wrinkled up her forehead and started thinking about Teddy Watson. "It's pretty mixed up," she reported after a while. "He seems to be thinking about a lot of different things. He's wondering if his mother will let him set up his electric train in the living room after they take down the Christmas tree, and he's trying to remember where he left his new fur mittens, and he's wishing the rest of the family would wake up so he could have breakfast, and he's wondering if he could set up his pup tent in his room and then light his Sterno stove and cook some pancakes without waking up his mother and father and have them come in and spoil it."

"That sounds like Teddy Watson all right," Joe said. "He's always going off in ten directions at once. But say, Jenny, how far do you think you could reach, anyway? What's maximum range?"

"Try my cousin George in Agawam," Uncle Harold suggested. "He lives at 108 Shoe Street."

"I'll see," Jenny said. Everyone sat still and watched her while she thought hard about Uncle Harold's cousin George. "He's not thinking very much," she said. "Just that he wished his head didn't ache, and why did he stay up so late seeing the New Year in, and then there was this girl at the dance—"

"OK, OK," Uncle Harold said hastily. "That was George all right. You can reach Agawam, I guess. Now we ought to try to find what your maximum range is. Let's see, I've got a friend in Bronxville that—"

"But Harold," Mrs. Pearson said, "give the girl a chance to eat her breakfast. She hasn't had a thing yet. You can try out her range afterward. My goodness, you wouldn't want her to try to reach all the way to Bronxville on an empty stomach, would you?"

After breakfast they tried Jenny out on the friend in Bronxville, and she reached him without any trouble, and then she listened in on her Aunt Isabel in Milwaukee, and tried to get Andy McDougal, the boy who had moved out West to Fresno, California, last year, but she couldn't hear anything there. Then they remembered that it was only about half past five out in California, so nobody would be up out there, or at least not thinking about anything.

Uncle Harold was fascinated, and kept trying Jenny out on all the friends or relatives he could remember, and Jenny was able to reach Tallahassee, Florida, and Little Rock, Arkansas, and Terre Haute, Indiana, and even Baggs, Wyoming. Stanley didn't think there was such a place as Baggs until Uncle Harold showed him on the map. That was where a classmate of Uncle Harold's had a sheep ranch, and Jenny reached him too. He was counting hay bales.

"How about trying somebody in Washington?" Joe said. "We ought to see what people are thinking about down there, since it's the capital of the country and all."

"Well, all right," Jenny said. "But I've got my dolls to take care of, and I haven't got time to sit around here all day. Why don't *you* think about someone for a change? Use your machines, why don't you?"

"But we can't do it," Joe said. "Our machines can't hear thoughts the way you can. Just this last one, Jenny, and then you can go."

Jenny shrugged her shoulders. "All right. Who shall I think about?"

"I don't know anybody in Washington," Uncle Harold said.

"Well," Stanley said, "maybe it doesn't have to be someone we know, but just anybody in Washington."

Joe looked at him scornfully. "But you've got to know *who* you're thinking about. It has to be some special person."

"All right then, have her think about the President. He's a special person. How would that do?"

"Now wait a minute," Uncle Harold objected. "This doesn't seem quite right. Do you think we ought to start prying into the President's thoughts like that? You know, he might be thinking about classified information or something, and we shouldn't listen in on it."

"But the President doesn't think classified thoughts *all* the time," Joe said. "We could try

Jenny on him, anyway, and if she starts getting classified thoughts, well, we can just turn her off again."

Uncle Harold looked doubtful. "Well, I'm not sure about this. It's kind of a new problem we've got here. But I suppose it wouldn't hurt just to try."

"Go ahead, Jenny," Joe said. "The President, in Washington."

Jenny turned her head a little to one side and listened. She began to smile.

"Well?" the others all said at once.

"He sounds just like Daddy," Jenny said. "There are three buttons missing on his shirt, and he thinks it's a fine state of affairs if he can't get his shirt washed without having all the buttons smashed off, and there's going to have to be a shake-up in the laundry department—"

"Well, I guess that wasn't classified," Uncle Harold said, looking relieved.

"Now how about the Queen of England?" Joe said. "This is going to be wonderful. We could reach anybody in the whole world."

"No, let's have Russia first," Stanley said. "We might find out their secret plans."

"But they probably think in Russian over there," Joe objected. "We wouldn't understand it."

"No. No more listening now," Jenny announced. "I'm going to take care of my dollhouse. The beds aren't even made yet."

"OK, Jenny," Joe said. "But take good care of your ear. That's just about the most important ear in the whole world."

CHAPTER NINE

THERE WAS cold weather all through the Christmas vacation, and the swampy pond at the bottom of the hill had frozen over hard, so there was good skating. Almost everybody played hockey, but Jenny's ankles were pretty wobbly, and she skated around the edge usually, where the weeds stuck up through the black ice. Teddy Watson hung around the upper end of the pond where the brook flowed in, seeing how far he could go on the thin ice before he fell through. When he found that out he climbed out of the water and went home. It was only up to his knees, so it wasn't very exciting, but there was a lot of mud, and that made it more interesting.

When it got dark everyone went home, and Mrs. Pearson let the three children toast marshmallows in the fireplace, because there was only one more day before school started. Stanley was on his fifth marshmallow when Jenny suddenly looked at him.

"That was Miss Griffin," she said.

"What was?" Stanley asked, reaching for his sixth.

"She just had the doctor come to look at her, because she fell down on her porch steps and hurt herself. The doctor says she cracked her sacrum, whatever that is. He said she would have to stay in bed for a while."

"How long?" Stanley wanted to know.

"About two weeks. She's mad, because she hasn't missed a day of school in fourteen years."

"Wonderful!" Stanley said. "Two weeks extra vacation for me! Good for Miss Griffin. She couldn't have timed it better."

"No such luck," Joe told him. "They'll get a substitute in, and you know who that will be. That's Mrs. Quigley."

Stanley was alarmed. "Oh, no! That would be worse than ever. She's *awful*. She hisses at you like a dragon. What can we do? We'll have to keep Miss Griffin on the job somehow. Maybe we can set up her bed in the classroom and she can live right there. Do you think they could do that? Keep tuned in on Miss Griffin, Jenny."

Joe shook his head. Then suddenly he and Stanley looked at each other. "The TV!" they both said at once.

Jenny was puzzled, because her left ear was busy listening for Miss Griffin. "What good will TV do?" she asked them.

"What good?" Stanley repeated. "It will keep away Mrs. Quigley."

"But how?" Jenny wanted to know. "Are you going to scare her?"

"No, no, Jenny," Joe said. "What we'll do is this. We'll take the TV set over to school, and set it up with the camera in the classroom and the screen in Miss Griffin's house, and she can watch what goes on in the classroom."

"I should think we'd want it the other way around," Stanley objected. "So we could watch Miss Griffin. You know, like those educational TV programs you hear about."

Joe didn't agree. "I don't think Miss Griffin would go for that idea. I think she'd much rather be watching you, than have you watching her. After all, there's not much chance that *she's* going to misbehave."

"Maybe you're right," Stanley admitted. "But it'd be nicer the other way. Well, let's go. We'd better start taking the TV down and packing it in a box."

"Wait a minute," Joe said. "Perhaps we ought to kind of clear this with the principal. We'd have to ask Mr. Billings about it before we began dragging in all that equipment. Besides, we'd have to persuade him not to get a substitute. That would spoil it all."

Jenny had been listening with her head turned. "You'd better hurry, then, because Miss Griffin has called Mr. Billings about her accident, and he's going to call Mrs. Quigley."

"Oh, wow!" Stanley said. "Quick, Joe, call up Mr. Billings and tell him our plan."

"Why not *you* call him?" Joe said. "It's your classroom."

"Oh, that's just the trouble. He'd think I had some special reason. He'd be suspicious. Come *on!* He'll call Mrs. Quigley in a minute."

They ran to the telephone, disconnected the automatic answering machinery, and called Mr. Billings's number. He answered right away.

"Hello?"

"Mr. Billings, this is Joe Pearson. We heard that Miss Griffin had an accident and wouldn't be able to come to school for two weeks—"

"How did you know that so soon, Joe? Miss Griffin only just called me about it."

"Oh—well, news travels fast, Mr. Billings. You know how it is. Word gets around."

"It sure does," Mr. Billings said. "Now was there something you wanted? I've got to make a phone call if you're through."

"Well, Mr. Billings, we thought that—I mean, we wondered if it wouldn't be a good idea to set up a closed-circuit television between Miss Griffin and her classroom, and then she could go right on teaching her classes, and there wouldn't have to be a change to a different teacher like if you had a substitute or something, and Miss Griffin would think it was better that way, and probably the class would too."

"Oh, no thank you, Joe," Mr. Billings said. "I don't think we need to do that. I was just going to call Mrs. Quigley now. She always substitutes when any of our teachers are out. So if you don't have any other questions, I'll go ahead with that. Thanks very much for your offer. Some other time, maybe. Good-by."

Joe made a wry face. "He hung up."

"But why did you give up like that?" Stanley said. "Why didn't you *argue* with him?"

93

"You can't argue with Mr. Billings. If you want to try it, go ahead."

Stanley looked gloomily out of the window. "Oh, beans. Two weeks of Mrs. Quigley. Maybe I could get sick or something."

Jenny held up her finger. "Just a minute, Stanley. I think Mr. Billings is going to call *us* up."

And right after that the telephone rang again. The three children pounced on it, but Stanley let Joe do the talking. He kept his ear close to the receiver, however.

"Hello, Mr. Billings," Joe said into the mouthpiece.

"Oh . . . er . . . hello. Is that you, Joe? This *is* Mr. Billings. I've just found out that Mrs. Quigley is out in St. Louis and won't be home for ten days. Now I didn't quite catch what you said about a television camera. Would you explain just what it was you had in mind, please?"

"Aha!" Stanley cried, and then clapped his hand over his mouth.

"Well, it's like this, Mr. Billings," Joe said. "You see, we have a closed-circuit TV system, and you can set up the camera in the classroom, and Miss Griffin can have the screen in her house, and she can watch what's going on in the classroom, and keep everything in order that way just as if she was there."

"I see," Mr. Billings said. "But how is she going to do any teaching that way? All she could do is watch. A teacher has to be able to talk to the class and hear what they say. What can we do about that?"

"Oh, that's simple, Mr. Billings. We'll just set up a two-way communication between her house and the classroom. We have all the equipment. We can just run the wires out the classroom window over to Miss Griffin's. It will be easy."

"Hum," Mr. Billings said. "I wouldn't do this sort of thing ordinarily, but Mrs. Quigley is our only substitute. Well, I'll call up Miss Griffin and see what she thinks about it. If it's OK with her, I'll drive up to your place about nine tomorrow morning. Can you have everything ready by then?"

"Oh, sure, Mr. Billings," Joe said. Then he hung up, and the two boys went into action. Jenny watched while they disconnected the TV camera and screen and packed them in boxes. Then they packed up some loudspeakers and microphones and a huge roll of wire, and put it all in the front hall for the morning.

Mr. Billings drove up the hill just before nine the next morning. He was a tall man, and always ducked his head from habit when he came through a doorway. He blinked at the pile of boxes.

"You sure you can put all this stuff together?"

"Oh, sure," the boys said. "We've had a lot of experience."

Up in the fourth grade room Mr. Billings helped them set up the TV camera on a shelf behind Miss Griffin's desk where it could look over the whole room. Then he left the two boys to fix up the wiring while he went back to his office.

Stanley frowned at the TV camera. "I think we ought to put the camera on the other side of the room. The way it is now it's got my desk right up in the front in full view. I'd rather be sort of off to the side more. If the camera was over on that side then Tina Marcelino would be in the front, and she's always well-behaved, and that would make a good impression."

"But then the camera would be pointing toward the windows, and the picture wouldn't be clear. You got to point away from the light, or it won't come out right. If the TV doesn't work pretty well Miss Griffin isn't going to like it, and then they'll give the whole thing up. So we've got to see that it works."

"Oh, sure," Stanley said. "I want it to work well, all right. I just didn't want it to work *too* well, that's all."

They hung the microphone from the overhead light in the middle of the room and put the speaker in one corner. They ran the wires out the window and stuffed up the crack with paper to keep the cold air out. Then they went to Mr. Billings's office and told him they would run the wires over to Miss Griffin's house, if he would bring the TV screen over in his car in about half an hour.

They borrowed a ladder from Mr. Bronson, the janitor, and fastened the wires to the elm tree in the schoolyard, then to a maple on the street corner and to another maple across the street, and then to a corner of the Doremus garage, and across their back yard to the Winslows' woodshed, and so on to Miss Griffin's brown house in the next block. Mr. Billings had already arrived, and they all helped to carry the television set into the house and up to Miss Griffin's room. She was sitting propped up in bed in a pink jacket.

"Well," she said. "Come in, Mr. Billings. How do you do, Joe and Stanley. I understand you're bringing me a television set, so I can go on teaching my fourth graders right here from my room. Isn't that wonderful? But I've never used a television

set before, so you'll have to show me all about it. Just put it right here on this table, where I can reach it easily."

They set it on the table, and the boys plugged in the wires. Then Joe showed her how to turn it on, and how to adjust the image. Then they connected the intercom with the speaker on the bureau and the microphone beside the bed.

"Now, turn it on, Miss Griffin," Joe said, "and we'll look at your classroom."

Miss Griffin turned it on. There were a lot of gray lines wiggling back and forth. "Heavens!" she said. "Is *that* my classroom? It wasn't like that when I left it."

"Now just a minute," Joe said. "You turn this knob till the image is right. There." The picture righted itself, and there was the classroom of Grade Four of Pearson's Corners School.

"Well, I *never!*" Miss Griffin said. "If that doesn't beat all! And what's that thing on that front row desk?" She pointed a long finger accusingly at the screen.

"Oh," Stanley said. "I guess it's my hat."

"And where does your hat belong?" Miss Griffin asked him.

"In the closet. I'd better go over and get it."

"And Stanley," Joe said, "when you get there we'll test out the sound and the camera position and everything. OK?"

"OK," Stanley said, and started out the door.

"Stanley!" Miss Griffin called after him. "What have you forgotten?"

Stanley put his hand up to his head, felt for his cap, then looked around the room, but didn't find it. Then his face grew red.

"Oh, I forgot to say good-by. Good-by, Miss Griffin."

"And?" Miss Griffin insisted.

"And Mr. Billings," Stanley said, and fled from the room.

"I don't know *what* to do about that boy," Miss Griffin said. "He just can't seem to remember what I tell him. He simply has no memory at all."

"Well," Mr. Billings said, "not about some things, perhaps, but he certainly can remember how to put all these wires together. He and Joe here just connected it all up in a jiffy. I was really impressed."

"Oh, wires, of course," Miss Griffin said stiffly. "But wires are quite another matter. I don't really believe in all this electrical business. It doesn't seem quite safe—or even natural."

"But it *is* helping us out of a tight spot," Mr.

Billings said. "It's a good thing in an emergency, I guess."

"Perhaps in an emergency," Miss Griffin admitted, "but I still don't like it."

"There's Stanley," Joe said, pointing to the TV screen. Stanley's image walked into the classroom and plucked up the hat from the front row desk. He said something they couldn't quite make out. "The volume's low," Joe said.

"Luckily," Mr. Billings added.

Joe turned up the volume knob on the speaker. "Can you hear me, Stanley?" he called into the microphone.

"Sure." Stanley's voice came back loud and clear.

Miss Griffin started. "Why, he sounds as if he were right in this room."

"Sit down in the back of the room, Stanley," Joe said. "And try talking from there. Just in an ordinary voice."

Stanley did, and the voice came through well at medium volume. Then they had Stanley write on the blackboard, but it was hard to read it. "They'll have to write in good large letters," Mr. Billings suggested, "but otherwise it works perfectly. We have to thank you boys for coming to our rescue, Joe— and Stanley," he added, turning to the screen.

"You're welcome," both boys said, only Stanley's voice came over the loudspeaker.

"Now you understand how to operate the equipment, Miss Griffin?" Mr. Billings asked. "In the morning you just turn on the set, and you'll see the children arriving, and you can take charge right from here. If there's any trouble, just call my office on the telephone, and I'll take care of it. All right?"

"I'll do my part," Miss Griffin said. "I can't speak for all this machinery." She was watching the screen intently.

"Fine," Mr. Billings said. "Now just call me if you need help. Good-by and good luck."

"Good-by, Miss Griffin," Joe said.

On the television screen Stanley's image came up close. He bowed stiffly and said, "Good-by, Miss Griffin." Then he made for the door.

"*Stanley!*" Miss Griffin's voice was stern. Stanley's figure turned, wondering, one hand on the door.

Miss Griffin pointed her long finger at the TV screen.

"Your hat," she said.

CHAPTER TEN

THE NEXT MORNING the three children started for school early. Joe and Stanley were eager to see how their first try at educational television was going to work out, and Jenny went with them. It was only three-quarters of a mile to school, but it wasn't so much fun walking by yourself. When they crossed the wooden bridge over Stony Brook they could hear the water running underneath the mounds of ice.

"How about tuning in on Miss Griffin?" Joe suggested to Jenny. "We ought to know how she's getting along. Is she going to remember to turn the switch on?"

"I'll see," Jenny said, and she stopped to listen. "She must be watching the TV screen already, because she sounds kind of impatient. It's eight o'clock already, she's thinking, and no one has turned the lights on in her classroom, and it's the first time in fourteen years that she hasn't been in her classroom at eight o'clock, and what will she do if no one can hear her when she talks over this microphone thing? She wonders how she can keep order when the class can't see her. She's worried."

"Well, anyway, I guess she's got things working," Joe said.

Mr. Billings met them in the hall by his office. "I locked up that classroom," he said, "because I didn't want anyone to get in there and fool around with that equipment, but now that you're here I'll get the janitor to unlock the door. And remember, we're counting on you two electronics experts to keep things running. If anything goes wrong, the system will break down, and I'll have to go in there and teach the class myself. That would be too bad."

"Yes, sir," Stanley agreed.

Mr. Bronson, the janitor, shuffled down the hall and unlocked the door for them. Stanley took off his hat and stuffed it firmly in his pocket before entering the classroom. As soon as he had gone through the door Miss Griffin's crisp voice came over the loudspeaker.

"Good morning, Stanley."

Stanley stiffened. "Good morning, Miss Griffin."

Then he hung up his coat in the closet and sat down at his desk, waiting for the pupils to come. Joe and Jenny went off to their own classrooms.

At eight-seventeen Jack Webster strolled in. His face lit up with delight when he saw the teacher's desk was vacant. "Hey, Stanley! Is it true that the Griffin broke something and can't get to school? Hot zig! I thought they were kidding me, but I guess it's true."

Stanley had been making fearful faces at him to warn him, but Jack ignored him. "That's great," he went on, sitting down on the corner of Miss Griffin's desk. "And I hear that Mrs. Quig—"

"Jack Webster!" Miss Griffin's voice crackled from behind him. "Get off my desk! And take off your coat and hang it up in the closet!"

Jack sprang off the desk and stood paralyzed. "And then sit down at your desk and start your arithmetic for today. Hurry up now. Don't just stand there with your mouth open."

Jack quickly hung his coat up in the closet and slid into his seat. He took out his arithmetic book and opened it, but Stanley could see his eyes turning this way and that, trying to see where Miss Griffin could be hiding. He couldn't seem to find her anywhere, so he wrote out "WHERE IS SHE?" in big

letters on his arithmetic paper, and held it up behind his book so Stanley could see it. Stanley didn't dare to point, but he looked up at the shelf where the TV camera was. Jack followed his gaze, but he couldn't see how Miss Griffin could be up on the shelf, so he looked back at Stanley with such a puzzled frown that Stanley couldn't help letting go a snort of laughter.

"Stanley!" the voice snapped. "You get busy. Haven't you enough work to do?"

"Oh, yes, Miss Griffin," Stanley said, all sobered down again.

Three girls came in and hung up their coats. They sat down at their desks and began looking around the room to see where their teacher was. They knew those two boys wouldn't be working that way unless Miss Griffin's eye was on them.

"It's no use looking for me, girls," Miss Griffin's voice announced, "because I'm not there. You may start in on your arithmetic, page eighty-one. Don't waste time."

The girls were mystified, but they got out their arithmetic books, and were stealing wondering glances at each other, when the rest of the class came crowding in the door. There was the usual bottleneck at the closet door, because eleven pupils in the closet were trying to get out at the same time that eleven pupils outside were trying to get in, but Miss Griffin's voice was precise and firm.

"Take your seat, everyone. Paul Burchard, you will lead the Pledge to the Flag, and after that Jeannette will take the attendance list to the principal's office. Then I shall give you the assignments for the day. I would not advise taking any liberties simply because you don't see me sitting at my desk, for I am perfectly able to see all of you. Now, Paul."

The class went smoothly for the rest of the day, and all that week. Wednesday afternoon the whole fourth grade came up to the Pearsons' house and sat around in the cellar for an hour. Stanley had said that they didn't want to be interrupted because they were going to study their spelling lesson.

"You're going to *what?*" Mrs. Pearson said, not believing her ears. But they didn't explain.

By Friday everyone was quite accustomed to instructions from the loudspeaker, and they all knew that Miss Griffin's watchful eye was on them even though she herself was two blocks away. Stanley even offered to set up an intercom between the classroom and Mr. Billings's office. Mr. Billings was pleased with the way everything was working.

"You know," he said to Miss McCallum after school on Friday, "it's just as good as having the teacher right there in the room. She can see everything, and hear everything, and talk to them all she wants to. And she keeps order there just as well as ever."

"Yes," Miss McCallum said. "She certainly does."

"I'd heard about this educational television idea before," Mr. Billings went on, "but I never realized it could work so well. And it has all sorts of other possibilities, you see. Now if a teacher had to be at a conference or something I could take her class right here from my office. In fact, it would be a good idea to have a camera in each classroom, and I could have a whole row of screens here in front of me, and I could see how things are going in any classroom in the building. We could supervise a class during its study period right from here, and that would give the teacher a chance to leave the room and do other things."

Miss McCallum brightened up at the idea. "I suppose it would be expensive, though, with all those machines."

Mr. Billings slapped his hand on his desk. "Not as expensive as teachers, Miss McCallum. You see, if a teacher can leave her classroom that way, she might as well be teaching in another room in her free time. If you arranged things right, one teacher could teach two classes. Maybe even three. It could save a lot of money."

Miss McCallum stiffened up a bit at that. "Then you could get rid of half your teachers, couldn't you? And the other half could work twice as hard."

Mr. Billings held up both hands toward her. "Oh, no. I didn't mean that, Miss McCallum. We wouldn't get rid of any teachers. Not at all. We just wouldn't have to hire so many new ones when the school gets bigger. It will be simply a more—well, a more efficient way of meeting the increased school enrollment, you see. Twice as many pupils, but the same number of teachers as before. Plus a lot of television screens. You understand what I mean?"

Miss McCallum said she thought she understood.

CHAPTER ELEVEN

"STANLEY," Mr. Pearson said at breakfast a week later, "I was talking with Mr. Billings yesterday."

"Yes?" Stanley said, helping himself to the strawberry jam.

"Yes," Mr. Pearson went on. "He came in to the store after school on Friday to buy a pair of pliers and a screwdriver. Said he was going to simplify things in his office. I asked him how the TV had worked out in the classroom. And he said, 'Thank the good Lord, Miss Griffin will be back on Monday.' He looked pretty done in, too, as if he had had a tough week. I told him it must be a help to get Miss Griffin back, but wasn't it a handy thing to have that electronic stuff in an emergency? 'In an *emergency!*' he said. 'That *stuff* is an emergency. Never again!' Then he took the pliers and walked out, shaking his head. What do you think of that?"

111

Stanley looked interested, but concentrated mainly on his piece of toast.

"I was wondering," Mr. Pearson said. "What could have put him in such a state? Wasn't the educational TV a success, Stanley?"

"I think it was a success—in some ways," Stanley said. "A few hitches here and there, perhaps, but pretty much a big success."

"But Mr. Billings didn't seem to think it was."

Stanley shrugged his shoulders. "Well, I guess from where he was he couldn't get the full benefit of it."

Joe Pearson spluttered when he heard that, and his father looked back and forth between the two boys. "There's evidently more to this than meets the eye. Just what *did* happen in school anyway?"

"You might as well tell him, Stanley," Joe said. "After all, I don't think Mr. Billings will want to use our equipment again for quite a while. Go ahead and tell how it was."

"Well, it wasn't anything very terrible," Stanley said modestly. "We cut out most of social studies every day by putting up a *Service Temporarily Interrupted* sign in front of the camera, and all we had to do was to pull it off the shelf with a string, and it hung down in front of the camera. That

112

cut off the view, and we knew we couldn't be seen."

"But I should think Miss Griffin would have reported that to Mr. Billings," Mr. Pearson said. "Why didn't he catch you at it?"

"Because we could hear whenever Miss Griffin called him up on the phone. Then Richard LaBonte would snatch off the sign and crawl back along the floor, out of range of the camera, and slide back into his seat. Andy Zwillinger would kind of lean over to one side to hide Richard's empty desk. It worked very well. We never had any trouble with it. But that business on Wednesday afternoon was Richard LaBonte's idea. I thought that was going too far. It might of put a stop to the whole thing."

"What was that?" his father wanted to know.

"Well, we planned out ahead of time that when the oral arithmetic began we would all talk softer and softer until finally we weren't making any sound at all. That would make Miss Griffin think that the speaker wasn't working. Then Richard had her turn her volume up full, and then we spoke up good and loud. She didn't sound like herself for the rest of the day. But she almost gave up the whole thing right there. And we had the best part still to come. I *told* Richard it wasn't a good idea."

"You mean there was *more?*" Mr. Pearson said.

"Oh, yes. Last Wednesday afternoon the whole class came up here to the house and we made a tape recording of our oral spelling test. Rebecca Worthen was the leader this week, and she asked the words, and we just spelled them out of the book. It took us about an hour and a half to tape it, but it was worth it."

"So that's what you were doing in the cellar," Mrs. Pearson said. "I couldn't believe my eyes when I saw you all trooping down there with your spelling books. I figured that if educational television could get a whole class to study their homework like that —well, then it really was a miracle."

Mr. Pearson was puzzled. "But what did you want to record your spelling test for? Just for practice, or what?"

"For *practice?* Oh, no," Stanley said. "We recorded it so we could have some time off in school. When it was time for the oral spelling lesson on Thursday, we just switched on the tape recorder, pulled the *Service Temporarily Interrupted* sign down over the camera, and then we had the period free for—well, for recreation, you might call it. We appointed Tina Marcelino to monitor the intercom and the warning system, so she could tell us

114

when to get back to our seats. We had just one strict rule, and that was that no one should make any noise above a whisper. And so, the tape recorder went ahead with the spelling test, while we played gin rummy in the back of the room and sailed paper gliders out the window. Andy Zwillinger tried to drop a water bomb on Mr. Bronson, but it missed. A little while after that, Tina heard Miss Griffin talking about us over the telephone and she warned us, and we all got back in our seats and switched off the tape recorder and put away the *Service Temporarily Interrupted* sign, and went on with the spelling test ourselves, so everything was OK when Mr. Billings looked in. He looked so disappointed that it was pretty hard not to laugh, but nobody did."

"So he didn't catch you at it?" Mr. Pearson said. "No wonder the poor man looked so worn out yesterday. You know what I would have done, if I was Mr. Billings? I would have just walked in on your class without any warning. Then you'd see what would happen."

"Yes," Stanley said. "That's what Mr. Billings decided to do. We kept Jenny tuned in on Mr. Billings all week so she could warn us if he made any plans like that."

"You mean Jenny had to listen to Mr. Billings's thoughts all that time?" Mrs. Pearson said. "How did she have time to do anything else?"

"Oh, we only asked her to do it in the daytime," Stanley reassured her. "We gave her time off for sleeping at night."

"Well, I should hope so," his mother said. "I thought Jenny looked awfully absent-minded lately, walking around with her head tilted on one side, not paying much attention to anything around her. I just thought she was growing up."

"I was very busy listening," Jenny told her. "I was listening so hard to Mr. Billings that I didn't always hear what Miss Romaine was saying in class. One time she asked me a question and I just said right out loud what I heard Mr. Billings thinking, and that was 'We'll have to have another first grade teacher next year,' and Miss Romaine looked kind of shocked for a minute, but then she understood, I guess. She said she'd be glad when I go back to hearing one thing at a time."

"Anyway," Stanley went on, "Jenny tipped me off that Mr. Billings was thinking of walking in on us suddenly, so I stayed in the classroom after school Thursday, and when I heard Mr. Billings talking to someone about how he was going to

116

surprise us the next day, I just got that all on the tape recorder."

"How could you hear him talking, though?" Mr. Pearson wanted to know. "His office is way down at the other end of the building."

"Sure it is, but we bugged his office when we put in the intercom, so we could listen in any time we wanted."

"You *whatted* his office?"

"*Bugged* it," Joe explained. "That means you slip a microphone into the place somewhere where he can't see it."

"I put it in his desk lamp," Stanley said, "and ran the wires out into the hall with the intercom wires, and he never noticed the difference."

"Now look here," Mr. Pearson said. "That's his private office. That's going *too* far. You boys don't know where to stop with your electronics. Just because you have a TV set doesn't give you the right to do anything you want."

"You shouldn't have done it," Mrs. Pearson said. "It's just plain eavesdropping, that's what it is."

"I don't see what's so wrong about it," Stanley said. "Even the FBI does it. And I used our best high-fidelity microphone too. It came through beautifully."

"But what good would that do you?" Mr. Pearson asked. "He could still come in and surprise you, couldn't he?"

"Oh, but we *behaved* ourselves on Friday," Stanley said, "because we knew he was going to pay us a visit. We checked with Jenny about the time, and we had the tape recording all ready to go, and just when he reached the door, we switched it on, and he opened the door and listened to himself saying he was going to surprise us. You should have seen his face. It was *something!*"

"I can imagine," his father said. "But there's something I still don't understand. How did you know the exact moment he was going to drop in on you? How could you tell when he was going to open the door?"

"That was easy. We had a photoelectric eye set up in the hall near his office door, and whenever he started down the hall toward us, a red light would go on in our classroom. We'd timed him before, and we knew it took him twenty-eight seconds to cover the distance, and so we could follow his course by the classroom clock. We jumped the gun by a couple of seconds, but I think that was because he listened outside the door before he opened it."

"A photoelectric eye? But I should think that would have set off your signal for anybody that went by in the hall. How could you tell when it was Mr. Billings?"

"But we put it on the top shelf of the display case in the hallway, and that was over everybody's heads except Mr. Billings's, so it wouldn't set off the signal except for him. Though one time Mr. Bronson went by with a broom over his shoulder, and that set it off. That was the only false alarm, though."

"Poor Mr. Billings," Mr. Pearson said, shaking his head sympathetically. "It'll be a long time before he tries anything like *that* again. I should have warned him it was dangerous to let you two move in your equipment."

"And he already has enough to worry about, poor man," Mrs. Pearson added. "He told us at the last PTA meeting that there would have to be another first grade next year, and he doesn't know where to put it. The only place he can think of is the old coalbin, that hasn't been used since they converted to an oil furnace. But that only has one little window."

"He'll have a lot bigger problem than that pretty soon," Mr. Pearson said. He was looking out the window, and from where he sat he could see all the way down the hill to the brook. There was an oblong of dark ice where skaters had shoveled away the snow.

"Why, Ed," his wife said. "You look so sad all of a sudden. What's the matter?"

"Oh, nothing. I was just thinking that . . . that I wanted the last piece of toast, and then Stanley took it."

Jenny was looking at him closely. "That wasn't what you were thinking about, Daddy."

"Why, of course it was, Jenny. It was a fine piece of toast, too, and all evenly buttered, and I was just thinking how nice it would taste, when Stanley scooped it up."

Jenny shook her head slowly. "No, Daddy, you weren't thinking that. I *know*. Is he really going to do that? The whole place?"

"Come on, Pop," Joe said. "You might as well tell us, or Jenny will."

"I suppose so," his father said. "There was a time when a man could have his thoughts to himself, but that seems to be impossible now. The trouble with Jenny's ear is that whenever I think about something, right away it's everybody's business, so I don't dare think about anything at all, hardly."

"I won't tell if you don't want me to," Jenny said.

120

Mr. Pearson sighed. "Well, you'd all have to know about it sooner or later anyway. So I might as well let you know now. It's simply this. Mr. Watson's going to move to Florida—you know that already—and he's going to sell his land here for small house lots."

"He *is?*" Mrs. Pearson said. "But who would buy house lots here in Pearson's Corners?"

"Plenty of people, according to him. He's talked it over with the State Highway Department, and they told him they're planning to put in a highway from Holyoke to Woronoco to connect with route 23 to Great Barrington and it will pass just south of Pearson's Corners, and the road from Westfield is going to be improved, and with the Massachusetts Turnpike so close we'll be right on the map. And so many people in Holyoke and Westfield are looking for homes outside the city that they'll buy up house lots almost anywhere if they're not too far away. And Pearson's Corners is about six miles from Westfield and ten from Holyoke, and with the new roads they can drive in to work easily. Anyway, that's the way Mr. Watson figures it, so he's going to go ahead with his plans."

"What about the hill?" Joe asked. "What will happen to that?"

"The hill will be covered with houses, I guess."

"And no more sliding?" Stanley said. "That would be awful!"

"But the brook will still be there," Jenny said. "We can still play in the brook, can't we?"

Mr. Pearson reached out and patted Jenny's arm.

"You always liked that brook, didn't you, Jenny? Do you remember when you were three years old, you walked all the way down there by yourself and fell in? It was only a foot deep, but you got wet all over. I tried to give you a scolding for it, but somehow I couldn't put my heart in it. Do you know why?"

Jenny looked at him for a while. "Because you did the same thing when you were little."

"That's right, Jenny. And I remember old Hiram Phelps was mowing at the bottom of the meadow and he fished me out of the brook with his rake, and took me back up to the house. And *my* father gave *me* a spanking, I remember very clearly. But later my grandmother told me that *he* had fallen into the brook when he was little. So you see, it's been an old family tradition. It's almost like being baptized."

Jenny had been watching him closely, a frown

growing on her face. "You mean they're going to take away the brook?" she said suddenly.

Mr. Pearson was very busy cleaning out his pipe.

"Well, perhaps not take it away, exactly, but they're going to put in drainage pipe and cover it over, so you won't be able to see it any more. But of course the brook will still be there, naturally."

"But it won't be much use if we can't get at it," Stanley said.

"How much are they going to cover up?" Joe wanted to know.

"Oh, from the bridge down to where it flows into the woods."

"The whole *thing?*"

"Well, yes," Mr. Pearson admitted.

"And that means," Joe said slowly, "that there won't be any more sliding *or* any more skating. Oh, great!"

"And no more brook to play in in the summer," Jenny said.

"Why do they have to cover up the brook, anyway?" Stanley asked. "What's wrong with having a little brook there, even if you did have houses all over the place?"

"Well, Mr. Watson says that he can get a lot more

house lots out of it if they drain the pond and cover the brook. And people from the city don't like brooks anyway, he says, because they're afraid their children are going to fall in and drown."

Jenny suddenly ran to the window and pressed her forehead against it and looked out on the hillside. When she turned back her mouth was down at the corners and there was a tear halfway down her cheek. "No more brook?" she asked, and her voice was unsteady.

"But Jenny," her mother said, "there will be a lot of new friends to play with. It will be very exciting to have all the new neighbors."

"And new business for Pearson's Hardware Store," Mr. Pearson said. "Think of all the lawn mowers and snow shovels we'll sell."

Jenny looked sadly at him, but didn't say anything.

"Well," Mr. Pearson said, just to break the silence, "maybe it won't be so terribly bad. I mean, lots of other people don't have hills and brooks near their houses, and they get along somehow. I don't know how, but they do. And after all, I suppose Henry Watson can sell his land if he wants to."

"Of course," Mrs. Pearson said. "But it does seem a pity he can't leave a little brook. Just think of all

those wild iris by the pond and the forget-me-nots along the edge of the brook. I shouldn't think he'd have to cover all that up."

"Well, gee whiz," Joe said. "What's the use of just sitting here and moaning about it? We ought to *do* something. We can't let Mr. Watson take away the sliding *and* the skating *and* the brook *and* the flowers and *everything*."

"That's fine, Joe," Mr. Pearson said, "but what do you aim to do? He's pretty much made up his mind, and he's a hard man to argue with."

"Well, maybe we could buy the brook from him, and maybe part of the hill."

Mr. Pearson shook his head. "I asked him about that, and he said he didn't think it would work out, having us own a strip of land running down the hill. It would interfere with the streets, he said. And having a pond there would scare away his customers, he thinks, so all he could suggest was that we buy the whole property—"

"Why don't we do that, Pop?" Stanley said.

"—the whole property for fifty thousand dollars," Mr. Pearson continued. "When I said we couldn't do that, he offered to buy our house if we decided to move away."

Nobody said anything for a while. Then Joe

looked up. "We ought to be able to raise fifty thousand dollars if we really put our minds to it. It just takes a little thought. Now let's see," he said, and his eyes moved slowly around the room. His gaze rested on his sister, and his mouth slowly came open.

"*Jenny*," he said, as if surprised at his own genius.

CHAPTER TWELVE

"WHAT DO YOU MEAN?" Mr. Pearson asked. "Where do you think Jenny's going to find fifty thousand dollars? Why, she hasn't even turned seven yet."

"Well, it isn't a question of how *old* she is," Joe said. "It's what she can *do* that counts."

"But, Joe," his mother said, "what can Jenny do that would earn all that money? She's too young even to be a sitter for the neighbors."

"Mom, you don't understand what I mean. Jenny can do something that no one else can do. She can read people's thoughts."

"Hum," Mr. Pearson said, filling his pipe with tobacco. "She'll have to read an awful lot of thoughts to make that much money. They just don't come that high nowadays. Besides, a fellow can read his own thoughts for nothing, so why should he pay some one to do it for him?"

"Well, you just wait and see," Joe said. "I think we can fix it so that Jenny can earn a lot of money. It's just a question of figuring out how to get started. And I've got an idea how to do that."

Jenny looked at him. "But I wouldn't be able to do that, Joe."

"Sure you could," Joe said.

"But I can't hardly spell *any* words. Just dog and cat."

"Aha!" Stanley said. "I see what you mean, Joe. I think you've got something. And then we could—"

"Wait a minute!" Mr. Pearson said. "What is all this anyway? I lost track of the conversation a long way back. There's too much mental telepathy around here for an honest man to keep up with things. Now what is this idea of yours, Joe?"

"Well, we could put Jenny in the town Spelling Bee week after next, and if we can work it right, she ought to be able to win the prize."

"But how?" Mrs. Pearson said. "Jenny can't spell against all those grownups. You know that, Joe. Why, old Mr. Whittier hasn't missed a single word for nine years. He has a photographic memory. How could Jenny beat him?"

"With *our* system, Mom, Jenny could beat anybody, even Noah Webster himself."

"Oh? What is your system?"

"Simple. I'll just bring the dictionary with me, and when Jenny's asked a word, I'll be sitting up in the audience, and I'll look it up for her, and she can read my thoughts."

Mrs. Pearson looked doubtful at this. "But Joe, do you think that's honest? That seems to be taking an unfair advantage of the other people in the Spelling Bee. After all, they don't have Jenny's—well, her telepathic ear."

"But Mom," Stanley said, "Jenny doesn't have a photographic mind like Mr. Whittier, and so why is a photographic mind any fairer than a telepathic ear?"

"Because it's—well—I don't know," his mother said. "What do you think, Ed?"

Mr. Pearson blew a cloud of smoke up toward the ceiling. "I guess Stanley has a point, perhaps. But assuming that Jenny does win the Spelling Bee, what good will that do? There's a ten dollar prize and a Webster's unabridged dictionary to the winner. Now let me see, ten into fifty thousand goes five thousand times, so in five thousand years we could buy that hillside from—"

"But that's not the *plan*," Joe interrupted. "The Spelling Bee is just the beginning—just a way to

130

get Jenny into the news, sort of. After that there's a kid's quiz program on that Westfield radio station, though that doesn't pay very much money, but then she could get on one of the big TV quiz shows after people begin to really hear about her, and then she can make *thousands* of dollars."

"Sure," his father said. "And you'll be sitting in the audience with twenty-four volumes of the encyclopedia on your lap. I can just see you now."

"He wouldn't have to be in the audience, Pop," Stanley said. "He could just sit right here at home and follow the program and whenever Jenny was asked a question he could look up the answer and she could reach him, even if she was in Boston or New York."

Mr. Pearson took a few puffs on his pipe. Then he looked across the table at his wife. She shrugged her shoulders.

"Well," he said. "It probably wouldn't do any harm to try the Spelling Bee, anyway. But if I were you I wouldn't expect too much from this. It seems a little too tricky to be very dependable. But go ahead with the Spelling Bee if you want to, and if Jenny wins it, it will be the first time in history that a Pearson ever did. I'm sure we won't object to the ten dollars, and an unabridged dictionary would be very useful. And it would be handy to hold down the kitchen linoleum when I glue it again."

"OK," Joe said. "Now let's see. We have to enter Jenny's name in the Spelling Bee before Saturday, don't we? And who do we speak to about that?"

"Mr. Billings," his father said.

"Oh? Well, maybe you or Mom had better tell him. I kind of think we'd better keep out of Mr. Billings's way for a while. He might think there was something queer about it if we were mixed up in it."

"And he might be right, too," Mrs. Pearson said.

The Pearson's Corners Annual Spelling Bee was always held the first Friday in February. It took place in the Town Hall, and always began at seven o'clock in the evening, so that the children wouldn't be kept up too late. In the last few years the attendance had fallen off bit by bit. Old Mr. Whittier said that the respect for good spelling was the backbone of our country and the *de*cline of the old-time spelling bee was a sign of the *de*cline of the American character. "When I was a young feller," he said, "the man who won the Spelling Bee made a name for himself, and he was respected, whether he was old or young, rich or poor. Why, sometimes *women* would win, and we'd even respect them."

But there were plenty of people in the Town Hall for this Spelling Bee. When the news got around that Jenny Pearson had suddenly shown a genius for oral spelling and was going to stand up against all the best spellers in town, even Mr. Whittier himself, everybody wanted to see what would happen. It was a snowy night, and people came in stamping the snow off their overshoes and shaking their coats. The two coal stoves in the meeting room were glowing red, and the room was pretty comfortable. There was such a crowd that there was scarcely room for everyone, and they had to set up some planks between chairs for extra seats. The contestants all sat up on the stage at the front of the room, and Jenny looked very small, sitting between Hank Baum and Mrs. Wilson. Hank had always been a good speller in high school, and he had come back from the University of Massachusetts to be in the Spelling Bee. He had big hands that stuck way out from his sleeves and some of his friends were betting on him for second place. Mrs. Wilson was a big, round, cheerful woman. She bulged out comfortably over the edge of the chair, and she always held on to her elbows when she was sitting down. She never could understand how she happened to be a good speller. She guessed she just couldn't help it. Last year she had come in second, and after fighting it out with Mr. Whittier for eleven turns had gone down with the word *portulaca,* which she had spelled with two *c*'s.

There were fourteen contestants in all, and Mr. Billings was the spelling master. He had a great list of words, starting with fairly easy ones and working up to the almost impossible kind at the end. When it was time to start he banged on the table and announced the rules of the contest, that each contestant would have one minute to spell his word, the first spelling would be final, and of course there was to be no whispering or signals from the audience. Everybody knew the rules by heart, but it was part of the ceremony, something like saying grace before a meal.

And then the Spelling Bee began. The first word was *buccaneer,* and it went to Miss Thorndike, who was a fast crisp speller, but with a tendency to get rattled on the really long words, like *extemporaneousness,* for instance. She had no trouble whatever with *buccaneer,* and the next word went to Peter Gustafsen, who worked down at the sawmill, and so on down the line. Mr. Billings gave Jenny the word *mosquito,* and the audience grew suddenly very quiet. Jenny wasn't very nervous about it, because she had practiced hundreds of times with Joe, while Stanley watched the clock, and she knew Joe could find any word in the dictionary within twenty seconds, no matter how long it was, and the rest was just a matter of listening to him think the letters. Joe quickly found the word, and while the audience watched her, she slowly and calmly spelled out *mosquito*. There was some clapping, and people turned and smiled at each other, and said "What do you think of that?" and "Well, I never!" to each other.

Mr. Billings kept on handing out words up and down the line of contestants. Peter Gustafsen dropped out on *penicillin,* and Ernie Greenspan missed *promissory,* so there were twelve people left. Then the words got harder. Sandra Williams missed the *a* in *dermatology,* and Mr. Marcellino slipped on *farinaceous.* Then Jack Lefevre left out one of the *r*'s in *corroboration,* and when the same word went on to Miss Thorndike she got upset, and put in an extra *r* that shouldn't have been there, so she was out.

Soon there were only four people still in the contest. Hank Baum staggered on *ineffaceable.* He wrestled with himself over the second *e*, gripped his hands together until the knuckles were white, and

135

his forehead glistened with perspiration, but he finally decided to leave out the *e*, and so he went down, shaking his head good-naturedly. He got a big hand from the audience. Jenny all this while had been spelling her words so calmly and slowly and steadily that the spectators were beginning to think she might even give the durable Mrs. Wilson a run for her money. And Mr. Billings gave out word after word, and still the three contestants went on spelling them correctly, and everyone was mystified at Jenny's new-found ability. And then when Mrs. Wilson, with her hands still on her elbows, spelled *muezzin* with one *z*, and Jenny spelled it properly with two, the crowd couldn't keep back their surprise. Mrs. Wilson gave a great laugh and reached over and congratulated Jenny with a thump on her back, and everybody cheered loudly.

That left just the two of them—old Mr. Whittier, with his big drooping mustache, dignified and confident in his photographic memory, and Jenny, sitting up straight and her feet not quite touching the floor. Everyone knew of course that Mr. Whittier was unbeatable. Why, the man had all those words in his mind just as clear as if they were on a printed page. But little Jenny there, well, she must be just a born spelling genius, an amazing

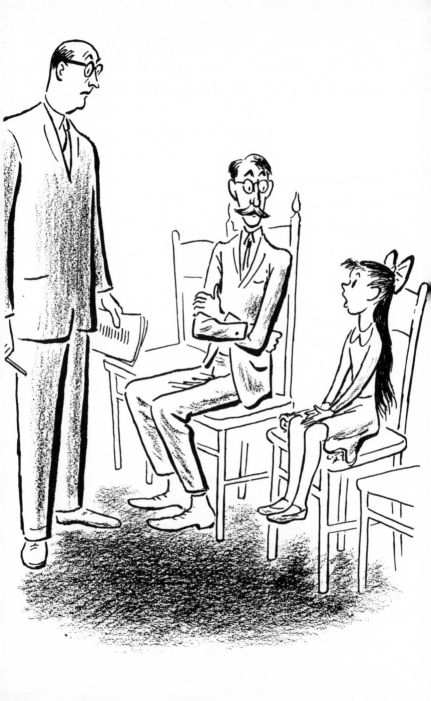

thing, particularly in the Pearson family, who were notorious misspellers. After all, if she had gotten this far without a slip, maybe she could keep right on.

But on the very next word something seemed to go wrong. Mr. Billings had given Jenny *mnemonic*, and she sat there quietly for some time, as if waiting for an inspiration. Thirty seconds went by, and the audience grew worried. "Poor thing," Mrs. Berry whispered to Mrs. Porteus, "she's all tired out. She's been up there for an hour now. No wonder she can't think any more."

In the meanwhile Joe Pearson was in agony. He clawed wildly at the pages of the dictionary, but couldn't find *mnemonic* anywhere. *Nem . . . nim . . . neem . . . num . . .* it just wasn't there! What could he do? Forty seconds gone already. Poor Jenny! His mother and father looked at him anxiously, but couldn't help. Fifty seconds gone!

With ten seconds to go, Jenny turned toward Mr. Billings and smiled. "*M*," she said slowly, "*n . . . e . . . m . . . o . . . n . . . i . . . c.*"

"Right!" Mr. Billings called. The crowd cheered and clapped, while Mr. Billings, who couldn't help feeling suspicious about the Pearson family, scrutinized the floor of the stage very carefully to see if there weren't any wires leading to Jenny's seat. He couldn't see any, but it *was* a very strange thing.

He gave Mr. Whittier *philatelist,* which he spelled correctly, and then Jenny was given *physiognomy,* and she spelled it right away this time, without waiting at all. Joe and Stanley realized, of course, that she was now getting her letters straight from Mr. Billings's mind, and this was a great relief to them because the words were becoming *very* hard to find in their dictionary.

The battle went on for several more words, but the audience could see that Mr. Whittier was getting uneasy. He was more accustomed to spelling against people his own size, and having this little slip of a girl sitting across from him made him nervous. He'd seen some fairly good spellers in his time, but this girl was *too* good. She just spelled by instinct—long words that she couldn't have ever *seen.* It wasn't memory, he was sure of that. In some mysterious way she was just spelling by *ear.*

It was the mystery of it that unnerved him. It distracted him so much that he could not see the words clearly in his mind. He nearly slipped on *phthisic,* and this rattled him. The audience could see him tapping his foot on the floor. He was losing confidence fast, and when Jenny sailed through *monocotyledon* without even a pause, it made matters worse. Then when Mr. Billings gave him *synizesis*, he went all to pieces. He couldn't remember ever having seen the word. No letters appeared in his mind at all. He started on *sina,* stopped and shrugged his shoulders. When Mr. Billings nodded to Jenny, there wasn't a sound from the audience as she spelled out the word. Then Mr. Whittier got up and walked over to Jenny and shook her hand.

The audience burst out in a shout of applause. They clapped and clapped, for Mr. Whittier as well as Jenny, because he had taken his disappointment so well. When they quieted down finally, Mr. Billings presented the ten dollars and the Webster's unabridged dictionary to Jenny, but it was too big for her to carry, and so Mr. Whittier carried it down off the stage for her and gave it to her father. Then there was a lot more clapping, and people got up and began putting on their coats, and mothers began calling to their children, who were climbing over the backs of the seats in order to get out first.

As they went out, Joe and Stanley Pearson could see Mr. Billings walking all around the stage, looking behind the chairs, examining the walls and the floor. He was a very puzzled-looking man.

CHAPTER THIRTEEN

"WELL, that worked out all right," Stanley said at breakfast the next morning. "That makes a very nice start."

"Yes, indeed," his father said. "That leaves us with only 49,990 dollars to go. At this rate—"

"But we're not going to go at *this* rate," Joe said. "The next thing is the children's quiz show at the Westfield radio station. We've watched that on TV over at Teddy Watson's. As soon as they read about what Jenny did at the Spelling Bee, they'll want her for their show. What day does *The Westfield News* come out?"

"Tuesday," Mrs. Pearson said. "But what if they don't want her for the show?"

"Of course they'll want her," Stanley said. "If the radio station doesn't call us up on Tuesday, we'll call them. Why, Jenny's the biggest news around. She could make a hit out of any quiz show."

"And we discovered something new last night," Joe said. "Jenny found out she could get her answers from the person who's asking the questions. That's going to make things a lot easier. Stanley and I won't have to look up the information for her. That part was worrying me a bit, but now she can just sit there and listen to the quizmaster. He's got to have the answer right there in front of him, so it will be simple. She can answer any question that they've got an answer for. So we just can't miss."

Mr. Pearson knocked his pipe ashes into the flower pot on the window sill. "Well, all I can say is I wish I had your confidence. Fifty thousand dollars is a lot of money."

Tuesday afternoon Mr. Pearson brought home the copy of *The Westfield News* and put it on the kitchen table. "There's the paper," he called, "and you even made the front page."

The children all shot into the kitchen. They searched up and down the columns of print and finally found it at the bottom of the page.

WHO SAYS WE CAN'T SPELL?

Pearson's Corners had its annual Spelling Bee on Friday evening, and guess who won. It was little Jenny Pearson, aged 6, daughter of Mr. and Mrs. Edward Pearson. The contest had narrowed down to the nine-time champion, Mr. Merit Whittier, and his youthful opponent, Jenny, who was competing in the event for the first time. Mr. Whittier finally tripped on the word *synizesis*, which Jenny spelled without any difficulty.

Miss Eleanor Romaine, who is Jenny's first grade teacher, said she had not noticed any unusual ability in her pupil up to this time, and said she had no idea how to account for it.

The principal of the Pearson's Corners School, Mr. Roger Billings, admitted that he was "surprised," but added that he hoped this would be an answer to the critics of present-day educational methods, who have claimed that the present generation haven't been taught to spell as well as their parents and grandparents. "Our teachers put a lot of emphasis on good spelling," Mr. Billings said, "and I guess this shows that it works. We all take pride in Jenny's training and ability."

"That's good," Joe said. "I guess they can't help seeing that. Now we just wait for the telephone call."

"Remember," Stanley said, "we're her managers, and they've got to handle everything through us. *Both* of us."

"Of course. But maybe I'd better answer the phone, because I would sound a little older than you. If they heard your voice they might get suspicious and call the whole thing off."

Stanley objected to this. "What's wrong with my voice, I'd like to know? It doesn't sound any more suspicious than yours."

"What are you boys arguing about?" Mr. Pearson interrupted. "Nobody's going to call you up anyway. If you want to get Jenny on a program on a radio station you'll have to go have an interview with the people down there. You can't get anywhere by just sitting around waiting for people to call you up and offer you something on a silver platter. Now the first thing you have to do—"

The telephone rang at this point, and neither of the boys waited to hear what the first thing to do was. Joe got the phone first, because Stanley tripped on the rug in the hall.

"Hello?" Joe said, sounding as old as he could.

"Hello," a man's voice said. "This Mr. Pearson?"

"Er—yes," Joe answered.

"You have a little girl that won the Spelling Bee in your town last Friday? Her name's Jenny, isn't it?"

"Yes, that's right."

"Well, this is Sam Bradley at Station WESF in Westfield, and we wondered if you'd be interested in having Jenny come in next Sunday afternoon to be on our children's quiz show. She made quite a name for herself in your Spelling Bee, and we'd like to have her for our guest this week. What do you say?"

"OK—I mean, that would be fine."

"Good," the voice on the telephone said. "The show is at two o'clock on Sunday. Better come in by one-thirty so she can get acquainted before we go on the air. Do you have any idea what sort of things she's especially interested in? Flowers? Birds? Storybooks?"

"Sports," Joe said.

"Sports? You mean jump rope and marbles and that sort of thing?"

"No, real sports. Like baseball, you know, the Major Leagues."

"How old is the girl?"

"Six," said Joe.

There was a pause. "Just baseball?" the voice said. "Or other sports too?"

"*All* kinds of sports," Joe said.

"You mean basketball, boxing, golf, tennis, horse racing?"

"Yes," Joe said.

"Well, all right. We'll put her down for questions

on all kinds of sports. Sounds kind of queer though. Don't forget, Sunday at one-thirty."

"OK," Joe said, and put down the telephone.

"What's the prize money on the show?" Stanley asked.

"Don't know. He didn't say. But anyway, this is just to get Jenny known. After she's known, then we'll begin to get some offers from the big programs."

"Sure," Stanley agreed. "Now all we've got to do is get Jenny in to Westfield on Sunday."

They went back to the living room, and Mr. Pearson looked over the top of his newspaper at them. "Well, what did they say? Do they want Jenny on their program?"

Joe nodded. "Yes, they do, and we're supposed to get her to the studio by one-thirty on Sunday."

"Oh, that reminds me," Mr. Pearson said. "Your mother and I were thinking of driving down to Westfield to see her Aunt Wilma on Sunday. We'll probably leave about one o'clock, I should think. Would any of you kids be interested in a ride?"

"Yes. All of us," Stanley said. "That would be perfect."

"The only thing is," Mr. Pearson added, "the car's such a mess that I couldn't think of going into Westfield with it looking that way. Maybe we'd better postpone Aunt Wilma until after we've had a good rain and the car's looking better."

"Oh, we'll clean it, Pop. We'll do it Sunday morning before church."

"Well, that would be very nice," his father said. "I'd appreciate that very much."

Sunday morning the boys got up early and cleaned the family Plymouth before breakfast, and for once Stanley was all dressed when it was time to go to church. It was a bright day, and fairly warm for February, and people stood around the church door talking in the sunshine until it was time for the service to start. The Reverend Hardible preached a sermon with the title "You Can't Keep Secrets from God," and Stanley kept asking Jenny in a whisper what different people in the congregation were thinking about. They were thinking about some pretty funny things, and not many of them were thinking about the sermon. After a while Stanley gave up asking, and the three children stared out the window at the drops of water dripping off the tips of the icicles on the eaves.

After dinner Stanley and Joe helped with the dishes without even being asked, and they were all ready to go at a few minutes past one. The roads were bare all the way into Westfield, and Mr. Pearson let the children off at the studio and said they'd be back and pick them up around two-thirty after the program was over.

They went into the building and up to the second floor where the studio was. There was a door that said WESF-TV on it, and Joe opened the door a crack and peeped in, but he couldn't see anybody, so he opened the door all the way and they walked in. The first room didn't have anything in it except a table and some chairs, but just then a man in his shirtsleeves came in from another room.

"Oh, hello there," he said. "This must be Jenny. I'm Sam Bradley." Then he looked at Joe and Stanley. "Her parents couldn't come today?"

"They're visiting Aunt Wilma," Stanley said, "but we're her managers. I'm Stanley and this is Joe."

"Managers?" the man said, giving them a rather doubtful look. "Does she need to be managed? You make her sound as if she was a prize fighter or something."

Joe frowned at Stanley and shook his head. "We're her brothers," he explained to Mr. Bradley.

"And she's a very special sort of sister," Stanley added, paying no attention to Joe's warning signals.

"Of course, of course," Mr. Bradley agreed. "All sisters are very special to their brothers. Now come along and I'll show you where we have our quiz program." He led the way into another room with two big television cameras on wheels, and microphones hanging down from overhead, and black electric cables twisted around all over the floor. There was a table at one end of the room, with chairs around it, and another man in shirtsleeves was tacking up sheets of white paper on the wall.

"Hey, Steve," Mr. Bradley said, "it's time for the news broadcast."

The man who was tacking up the paper looked at his wrist watch and said "Wow!" and dashed out of the room, grabbing up his coat from the doorknob as he went past.

"You can see him on the monitor set," Mr. Bradley said to the children, pointing across the room to a TV screen. There was the man who had been tacking up paper, sitting calmly at a desk. "Hello, folks," he was saying. "Time for our five minutes of news and weather reports. The three-alarm fire in the rubber boot factory in Fitchburg is now under control, the Fire Chief says. Patricia Sinclair of Belchertown has been chosen Carnival Queen at the annual Dartmouth Winter Carnival in Hanover, New

Hampshire, and the Massachusetts Junior Ski Championships are being held today at the ski area in Otis. At Pittsfield, a haybarn collapsed—"

"Well, now," Mr. Bradley said, "This is where we have our quiz program. I sit at this end of the table, and you know what I think, Jenny?"

"Yes," Jenny said, but luckily Mr. Bradley didn't notice.

"I think I'll have you sit right there next to me. OK?"

Jenny nodded.

"And I'll ask some questions, and if you know the answers, just stick up your hand. And when you speak, remember to talk right up and don't mumble. And we'll let your—your managers sit right over there across the room where you can see them, and you won't feel frightened or anything like that, will you?"

Jenny shook her head.

"All right," Mr. Bradley said, "our show goes on in about ten minutes, so we'd better go out and meet the other experts on the program."

They went out into the other room, and there were four other children, all taking off their coats and overshoes. Two were girls and two were boys, and one of the boys wore dark horn-rimmed glasses, and had his hair all slicked back and looked very brainy, but not very nice, Jenny thought. She knew he was thinking that she was too little to be on a quiz program with him, and Jenny could tell that he was going to say that as soon as he got a chance.

Mr. Bradley introduced them all around. The name of the brainy-looking boy was Calvin something, and as soon as the introductions were over he pointed a finger at Jenny and said, "Is that little kid the guest expert today? What's her specialty? Nursery rhymes?"

"Nope," Mr. Bradley said. "Sports. But come on, kids, it's almost time to go on the air."

There were two cameramen in the studio now, one behind each camera, and as soon as they all were in their seats, Mr. Bradley raised his hand and pointed to the clock. Then he looked at the nearest camera and smiled. A red light went on over by the door. "Good afternoon, everybody," he said, still smiling. "Our panel of junior experts is gathered here for our regular Sunday afternoon quiz program. Most of the members you know already—Norma-Rae deRosa, down at the end of the table, Calvin Hooper next, then Carol Richfield, and John Anderson. And sitting next to me, ladies and gentlemen,

is our guest expert for today, Jenny Pearson, the little girl who won the Spelling Bee up at Pearson's Corners last week. This is quite an accomplishment for such a young lady. How old are you, Jenny?"

"Six," Jenny said.

"Six? And you outspelled all those grownups at the Spelling Bee? What do you think is the secret of your spelling ability? Do you read a lot?"

"A little," Jenny said.

"Well, it's a very strange thing. How do you suppose you were able to spell all those hard words?"

"I just listen." Joe and Stanley stiffened in their chairs at this, but Mr. Bradley went right on.

"Well, listening's a very good thing to do, Jenny. We'd probably all be much wiser if we did more of it. Now, we've been told that you are particularly interested in sports, so we're going to have some questions on sports today, and we'll see how good our experts are on that subject. You remember the rules, now. Raise your hand if you think you can answer the question. I'll call on the first person to get his hand up. If there's a tie, I'll hold up one or two fingers behind my back, and the one who guesses right can answer the question. All set?"

The experts all nodded.

"Then here's the first question," Mr. Bradley said,

looking at a card which he held in his hand. "Who won the World Series last fall and by how many games?"

All five children raised their hands, but Calvin Hooper's hand was definitely the first.

"The Yankees, four to three," Calvin announced, looking as if it was scarcely worth his while to answer such a simple question.

"Right. Now the next question. What was the score of the last Yale-Harvard football game?"

This time three hands went up, Jenny's and Norma-Rae's and Calvin's, but Calvin's was the first again.

"Yale 42, Harvard 14."

"Right again," Mr. Bradley said. "You're sharp today, Calvin."

Calvin nodded and looked over at Jenny with half-closed eyelids. Jenny could see that he was going to be hard to beat. And Joe had told her that she would have to make a good showing on this program if their plan was going to work. So, she decided she would have to do what she could.

"Third question," Mr. Bradley said. "Who won the Sixtieth Boston Marathon?"

This time Jenny was watching, and stuck up her hand when Calvin did.

"A tie," Mr. Bradley announced. "I have one or two fingers behind my back. We'll give our guest the first choice. Jenny, do you say one, or two?"

"Two," Jenny said without any hesitation.

"Two it is. Now what's the answer, Jenny?"

"Antti Viskari of Finland," Jenny said.

Everybody looked rather surprised, and Calvin Hooper looked angry. Sports was one of his specialties, and he hadn't expected to have this little girl get ahead of him.

The next question was: What cowboy is leading in all-around rodeo standings? This time Jenny's hand was up first, though Carol Richfield and Calvin were close behind.

"Yes, Jenny?" Mr. Bradley said.

"Jim Shoulders, of Henryetta, Oklahoma." That was the right answer, of course, and from then on Jenny answered all of the questions, no matter how hard they were. She reported that Ida Simpson of Buffalo, New York, was the Individual Champion of the Women's International Bowling Championships of 1951, and that Champion Kippax Fearnought was Best in Show in the 1955 Westminster Kennel Club Dog Show. Harvard, Jenny said, had won five of the last ten Harvard-Yale boat races, and Ted Allen of Boulder, Colorado, had been World Horseshoe Pitching Champion seven times. She also knew, apparently, that Krivonosov of Russia had made the world's record 16-pound hammer throw of 211 feet and one-half inch, and that Florence Chadwick held the England-to-France channel swim record of 13 hours, 55 minutes. There seemed to be nothing about sports that Jenny didn't know, and Mr. Bradley grew more and more amazed. He had saved a few almost impossible questions for the very end, just in case the experts had been able to answer all the others. He turned to these cards.

"Who was the winner of the 1944 Hambletonian Harness Stakes, and what was the time and prize money?"

Jenny put up her hand right away, as usual. "Yankee Maid," she said, "time, two minutes four seconds, prize money 35,577 dollars."

Mr. Bradley gulped, and picked up his last card. The other children were staring at Jenny with open mouths. "Well," Mr. Bradley said, "our time is almost up, and here's the last question: What was the weight and size of the world's record codfish caught with rod and reel, and where and when was it caught, and who caught it?"

Jenny was the only one to raise her hand for that one. She took a deep breath. "The weight was 57 pounds 8 ounces, length 4 feet 8 inches, and it was caught at the Ambrose Light off New York on December 24, 1949, by Mr. J. Rzeszewicz."

Mr. Bradley mopped his forehead with a big handkerchief. "Well, I've never seen anything like *this* before. It's been an amazing performance, Jenny, and the sponsor of this program, the Westfield Home Bakery, presents you with a giant-size package of their assorted cookies for appearing on our quiz program this week. And that's all until next Sunday."

The red light snapped off, and everybody began asking Jenny how she happened to know so much about sports at her age, but Joe and Stanley slipped in and rescued her. They explained that they didn't want to miss their ride home. Just before they went out the studio door, Mr. Bradley caught up with them.

"Say, kids," he said, "I think Jenny here has real talent. Now I've got connections with a big quiz show in New York, and they're always looking for really unusual talent like this. They've asked me to sort of keep an eye out for kids that would make good contestants. How would it be if I arranged for an interview sometime soon? Would you be interested?"

Joe took hold of Stanley's arm to keep him quiet. "Well, I think so," he said. "But of course we'd have to be careful of her. She's pretty young, you know."

"Oh, certainly," Mr. Bradley assured him, "they'd be very careful. Don't worry about that. But remember, don't sign any contracts or anything until you hear from me again. OK?"

"OK," Joe said, and they went down the stairs and out to the street. They waited on the sidewalk for their parents.

"That was *neat!*" Stanley crowed. "Did you see how that Calvin folded up when you started in, Jenny?"

Joe patted her on the back. "Jenny, you were wonderful. It was just perfect. They never even *guessed* how you did it. I was worried a couple of times when you started to raise your hand *before* he asked the question, but nobody noticed. And Mr. Bradley's a talent scout for a New York show, and everything's working out fine."

The familiar old Plymouth stopped just beside them, and they all piled into the back seat. "Well, how'd it go?" Mr. Pearson asked.

"Fine," Stanley said.

"It looked very impressive to us," Mrs. Pearson said. "We watched the program on Aunt Wilma's

TV set. I must say we couldn't help feeling proud of Jenny, when she answered all those hard questions, even though we knew she didn't really *know* the answers."

"She *did* know them," Stanley insisted. "She knew them by listening to Mr. Bradley's thoughts, and there's no law against mind reading, is there?"

"Not yet," his father said. "But maybe there will be soon."

No one said anything about prize money until they got home, but at suppertime Mr. Pearson asked how much Jenny had made on the show.

"A giant-size package of cookies," Joe said modestly.

"Why, that's splendid," Mr. Pearson said. "Now we have ten dollars, a dictionary and a giant-size package of cookies. We're really making progress toward that fifty thousand, and we have two whole months to go. I don't see how you can miss."

"Now Ed," Mrs. Pearson said, "don't be sarcastic. The children are really trying as hard as they can. The least we can do is to appreciate it."

"Sure, I appreciate it all right. I just want them to be realistic about it. We've got to show them the facts, or they're going to be terribly disappointed when things don't work out. After all, fifty thousand dollars isn't just hanging in the air waiting to be picked, you know." He looked around at the three children, who all were particularly poker-faced. "You know that, don't you, kids?" Mr. Pearson said.

"In the *air?*" Stanley repeated.

"You can never tell about things like that," Joe said.

CHAPTER FOURTEEN

THE NEXT EVENING, just after supper, there was a telephone call from New York for Mr. Pearson.

"Hello?" he said.

"Hello," a voice said. "Do you have a daughter Jenny, who appeared recently on a children's quiz program?"

"Yes," Mr. Pearson said.

"Well, this is Gladys Svelt, of the North American Broadcasting Corporation, and we have heard from Mr. Bradley in Westfield that your daughter has shown some unusual ability. Would you be interested in letting us interview her for possible appearance on one of our programs?"

"Why, yes, I would—that is, I think so. I'll have to ask her brothers—I mean, her managers."

"Managers?"

"Well, really her brothers. Just a minute, while I

ask them." He put his hand over the mouthpiece and turned to Joe and Stanley. "All right for Jenny to have an interview for another program?"

"What station?" Joe wanted to know.

"She said the North American Broadcasting Corporation."

"OK," Joe said, and Stanley agreed.

"Hello?" Mr. Pearson said into the telephone. "They said OK—I mean they said that it would be all right."

"Fine," Miss Svelt said. "And would the day after tomorrow be all right for an interview? That would be Wednesday the eighteenth."

"Well," Mr. Pearson said, "it may be hard to get Jenny down to New York on short notice like that. I'm shorthanded at the store, and I don't know that I could get away right now."

"Oh, you needn't do that," Miss Svelt said. "I'll come up to Pearson's Corners and interview Jenny in your home. Would three o'clock be a good time?"

"They don't usually get home from school until half past three," Mr. Pearson said, "but they could get out early for something important like this, I should think."

"All right," Miss Svelt said, "I'll come at half past three. Good-by."

Mr. Pearson came back to the living room. "You know, I find it pretty awkward having to clear everything with you two managers. People are going to think I can't make up my own mind."

"That's all right, Pop," Stanley said. "You did fine. And now we'll have a chance at the big programs. Things are really moving."

"But we've got to be careful," Joe warned. "We've got to see that things go right at this interview. One slip might queer the whole thing. We'll have to give Jenny a few tips about the interview, for instance. If she asks you to *write* anything, Jenny, be sure to write *awfully* slowly. Then she'll be more likely to have you answer questions out loud. And when she gives you a question, don't answer it right off, but look as if you were thinking it over, and sometimes look as if you could hardly remember."

"And be sure not to answer the question before she asks it," Stanley said. "That would be fatal."

The boys trotted all the way home from school on Wednesday, with Jenny riding on Joe's back most of the way, so she wouldn't be tired for her interview. When they got to their house, there was a huge yellow Buick parked by the mailbox. They were all a little nervous because this was going to be an important moment.

Miss Svelt was sitting in the living room talking to Mrs. Pearson. She looked around quickly when the children came in. She was wearing glasses with blue rims that came to a point at the ends, and her hair was pulled into a lump at the back of her head. Mrs. Pearson introduced the children to her.

"So this is Jenny," Miss Svelt said. "I've heard a great deal about you, Jenny. We've heard so much that we wondered if you would like to be on a television show with us. Would you?"

Jenny nodded.

"But of course the people we pick for our television shows have to be just right for that particular show, so we have to choose them very carefully. And if we found that you weren't just the right person for our show, you would understand, wouldn't you?"

Jenny nodded again.

"And so," Miss Svelt went on, "I brought along some questions to ask you, to see if we will be able to use you on a program. Now what sort of things are you interested in most?"

Jenny glanced at Joe and Stanley. "*All* kinds of things."

164

Miss Svelt smiled patiently. "Now that's very nice, of course, to be interested in everything, but I mean what sort of things do you know the most about? What are your particular specialties?"

Joe had told her that she would be asked this, so Jenny had her answer all ready. "I guess I know the same amount about everything," she said.

Miss Svelt could see she wasn't going to get anywhere with this kind of approach, so she opened up a notebook she had with her. She took out a sheet of paper with a lot of questions on it and handed it to Jenny. "Now if you just answer as many of these questions as you can," she said, "we'll find out what sort of things you're best at."

Jenny looked at the sheet of paper, and then glanced at Joe and Stanley. She studied the paper for a while. "I can't read very fast," she announced. "And I don't write very good. I'm only in the first grade."

"Oh, of course," Miss Svelt said. "What was I thinking of? Here, I'll read the questions to you, and you answer them out loud. But we mustn't have any hints from your brothers. Perhaps they ought to go into another room?"

"But they're my managers," Jenny said.

"We'll sit over here in the corner," Joe said, "and

we won't make a sound. Besides, Jenny's the one who can answer questions, not us."

Miss Svelt thought that over, and nodded her head. "All right, then, Jenny, here's the first question. What strange country of little people did Lemuel Gulliver visit on his first voyage?"

"Lilliput," Jenny said.

"Good. And here's the next question. This is harder. Do you know who wrote *Paradise Lost?*"

"John Milton."

Miss Svelt began to look surprised. "We'll have to try something even harder," she said. "Who wrote *Brave New World?*"

"Aldous Huxley."

"Good heavens!" Miss Svelt said. "You're an expert on literature. Now for some other fields. Science next. What is the diameter of the earth?"

"Seven thousand, nine hundred and twenty miles."

"How far is it from the sun to the earth?"

"Ninety-three million miles."

"And when was the safety pin invented?"

Joe made a warning motion with his hand for Jenny to slow down, so she paused before answering. Miss Svelt looked up from the question sheet. Jenny wrinkled her forehead and looked up at the ceiling. Finally she said, "1849."

"Correct," said Miss Svelt. "You seem to be an expert on science too, Jenny. Now let's see how you are on history. When was the battle of Marathon?"

"In 480 B.C."

"When did Mohammed flee from Mecca?"

"In 622 A.D."

Miss Svelt put down her paper. "Why, I've never seen anything like *this*," she said. "I'm *certain* we can use you, Jenny, and we'll let you know just as soon as we can what our plans are for you. And in the meantime, you won't go on any other TV show, will you?"

"By the way," Joe said, "Stanley and I were wondering what sort of prizes you can win on your shows."

Miss Svelt folded up her notebook. "We have a junior program, the 'Brain Child' show, that offers prizes of a trip around the world by airliner and a four-year college scholarship. It's a wonderful opportunity."

"But we need *money*," Stanley said. "Don't you offer any money prizes? The other broadcasting companies do."

"Oh, of course," Miss Svelt said quickly. Our 'What Do You Know?' program offers twenty-five thousand dollars in cash and a Cadillac convertible."

"Is that the highest prize?" Stanley said. "We need more than that."

"Oh, well," Miss Svelt said, "we do have our top quiz program, 'Beat Your Brains.' This has a prize limit of one hundred thousand dollars. But we've never had any children on that program."

"But you've never had any children like Jenny either," Joe pointed out. "I'm afraid we can't afford to let her take part in the smaller shows. We have to have our money in two months, and we can't waste any time."

Miss Svelt tapped the toe of her high-heeled shoe on the floor. "I'll have to discuss this with the directors," she said.

"All right," Joe said. "But let us know soon, because we have to go ahead with our plans."

"We'll call you tomorrow," Miss Svelt assured him. Joe helped her into her fur coat, and Stanley brought her fur-lined overshoes from beside the radiator. Mrs. Pearson came out of the kitchen to say good-by. They watched until the yellow Buick disappeared down the hill.

"That hundred thousand dollar show is the one for us," Stanley said. "We can buy the hill from Mr. Watson and have fifty thousand left over."

"Not quite," Mrs. Pearson told him. "Your father was talking to Mr. Watson yesterday, and he said that some real estate men had told him he ought to ask seventy-five thousand for his land. That's what he wants now."

"Oh," Stanley said. "But that's all right. We could pay that and still have twenty-five thousand dollars left over. What's twenty-five thousand one way or the other? How long does that show run, anyway?"

"Three weeks," Joe said. "That will give us plenty of time to win the top prize and pay Mr. Watson for the land. That is, if they start soon enough. And I just had a queer thought. Suppose Jenny's ear should suddenly conk out on us. What would happen then?"

"Why would it do that?" Stanley said. "Your ear's still all right, isn't it, Jenny?"

"Yes," Jenny said. "But it was all right before. I guess I can't tell what it may do."

"That's it," Joe said. "It came suddenly, and it might go suddenly. There wouldn't be any warning. We might find ourselves right in the middle of a program, and her ear would go dead, and then where would we be?"

"That would be bad," Stanley agreed. "Jenny, you've got to keep that ear going at least for another month. Try extra hard, won't you?"

"I'll do my best," Jenny said. "But I don't exactly know what to do."

Miss Svelt called on the telephone from New York the next day, and said that the producers of "Beat Your Brains" had agreed to put on Jenny for a three-week run beginning Friday, February 27. The questions were to be on general information, and the company was reserving hotel rooms for the Pearson family for each Friday night that Jenny was appearing, and the company would pay the train fares for the whole family.

"But what about school?" Mr. Pearson said doubtfully. "These kids will be out all day Friday, three weeks in a row. What's Billings going to think about that?"

"We can clear it with Mr. Billings," Joe said. "He's been feeling pretty good about us ever since he got mentioned in the paper after the Spelling Bee. And we can show him how much publicity he can get for his school if Jenny goes on a big show like this. He kind of likes publicity."

CHAPTER FIFTEEN

FOR THE NEXT WEEK Joe and Stanley coached Jenny in how to behave on a quiz show. They spent hours watching quiz programs at Teddy Watson's house in order to study the technique. "You don't want it to look too easy," Joe warned her. "You know all the answers just as well as the MC does, so you can answer the questions without any trouble. But the idea is make it *look* as if you were suffering —you know, racking your brains trying to think of the answer. First you should look sort of blank, as if you didn't have the vaguest idea about it, and then you put on a faraway look as if you had just thought of something but couldn't quite remember what it was. Then you squirm around and frown and act as if you had a terrible pain for a while, and then you suddenly light up and look pleased and rattle off the answer. That's the way the big quiz stars do it, and the audience gets to expect it that way. They'd be disappointed if you didn't."

"And kind of hesitate a little sometimes," Stanley suggested. "You don't want to sound too much like an encyclopedia."

Jenny did as she was told, and they would practice on all sorts of questions, like what is the highest waterfall in the United States, or what was Mickey Mantle's batting average in 1956, and Jenny got to be an expert at looking as if she were trying to find the answer.

And then came Friday, February 27, and the Pearson family drove down to Westfield and took the 9:43 train to New York. It was a gray morning, and it was snowing by the time the train got into New York in the middle of the afternoon. They climbed up the long ramp into Grand Central Station and stared up at the ceiling, and then they went out on the street and got in a taxi. The streets were all covered with gray slush, and people were hurrying from one place to another. The taxi took them to the Hotel Ambassador on Park Avenue, and Mr. Pearson signed up in the guest book, and a bellboy in a flat sort of cap took them up to their rooms. Joe and Stanley and Jenny leaned on the window sills and looked out over the square roofs. It was getting dark already, and snowflakes were floating past the lighted windows across the street.

Pretty soon the telephone rang. It was Miss Svelt, who wanted to tell them that a car would come for them at quarter to eight, and bring them to the studio. Jenny was supposed to have a nap until suppertime, because she was going to be up late at night, so they pulled down the shades and everybody went out and left her alone.

They had supper in the hotel dining room, and there were waiters dressed in black suits carrying dishes with metal covers over them, and the headwaiter came over and told them that their dinner was all paid for by the broadcasting company, and was this the young lady who was going to be on the quiz program? He bowed to Jenny and the rest of the family, and then went on to another table.

It got to be quarter to eight very quickly, and the car came for them, and they drove through the slushy streets and there were red and blue lights everywhere with enormous names like FIAT and QUO VADIS. When they got to the studio Miss Svelt met them and showed them the room where the show was going to be, and she explained to Jenny about the isolation booth where the contestants sit while they answer questions so no one will be able to give them any hints. Pretty soon it was almost time to begin, and Mr. and Mrs. Pearson and Joe and Stanley were shown to their front-row seats in the audience. Jenny began to feel a little nervous sitting up on the stage by herself, but just then Miss Svelt came in and introduced her to a shiny-faced man in a dark suit. He had dazzling white cuffs.

"This is Mr. Random Groper," she said. "He is the quizmaster for this program, Jenny, and I've asked him to do all he can to help you—except to give you the answers, of course."

Mr. Groper flashed a big toothy smile at her and reached out a hand to her. Jenny shook it and said, "How do you do?" She could hear Mr. Groper thinking. He was sure this was going to be a flop. He had told them and told them not to make this into a kid's program. No kids, he'd said to them. Politicians, lawyers—even poets, if necessary, but no kids on an adult show. And now see what they're giving him. Well, they'll soon find out—and they can't blame him if something goes wrong.

Almost at once the red light went on, and the program started. Mr. Groper now faced into the

175

bright lights and flashed his white teeth. "Good evening, ladies and gentlemen," he announced. "Once again we bring you the 'Beat Your Brains' show, through the courtesy of our sponsor, the Hopper and Leach Soap Company, makers of laundry soaps bearing the nationally known names of Drift, Weft, Sift, Soothe, Sloth, Froth, Spume, and now a new brand with the name Scud, with the new miracle ingredient Z-17, guaranteed to make your washdays brighter, longer and happier than ever before. Hopper and Leach also produces La Maja and Priscilla Alden hand soaps for ladies, and for men Scimitar shaving creams and Old Salt After-shave Lotion."

Mr. Groper paused and beamed out over the audience. "Now this evening, ladies and gentlemen, we have a *little* surprise for you. Up to this time, as you know, our experts on this quiz program have all been adults, but tonight we have with us a young girl—a *very* young girl—by the name of Jenny Pearson. How old are you, Jenny?"

"Six," Jenny said. "I'll be seven in April."

"And where do you live?"

"Pearson's Corners, Massachusetts."

"And that's up near Westfield, Massachusetts, isn't it?" Mr. Groper said, looking briefly at his script.

"Yes."

"And what's the population of Pearson's Corners, Jenny?"

"It's four hundred and seventy-three now, because the Zwillingers had a new baby last Tuesday."

"I see," Mr. Groper said. "Now do you realize, Jenny, that if you are able to answer all the questions that we put to you, you will be able to win the enormous sum of one hundred *thousand* dollars?"

"Yes," Jenny said modestly.

"I'd be interested to know," Mr. Groper went on, "what you would plan to do with all that money if you won it. Could you tell us?"

"I want to buy a hill," Jenny said.

Mr. Groper looked surprised. "A hill? Why do you want to buy a hill?"

"Because if I don't buy it it's going to have houses all over it, and then nobody can slide on it any more, and they'll cover up Stony Brook and there won't be any more skating or any flowers or anything."

"Well, well," Mr. Groper said, somewhat taken aback. "I'm sure we all hope you can buy that hill. Now, we'd better start on our questions. First, I'd like to explain how the 'Beat Your Brains' contest works. It's really a game of fifty questions. This evening we will ask you seventeen questions, and each one you answer correctly will win you one thousand dollars. Then next Friday we will ask you another seventeen questions. That means that by the second evening you could win a total of thirty-four thousand dollars. Then on the third Friday, we ask you *sixteen* questions, making a possible grand total of fifty thousand dollars. *Then* we ask you one more final question, and if you get *that* right, you can double your winnings, making a possible hundred thousand dollars in all. Understand?"

Jenny nodded.

"Now, we wish you good luck, and if you will step inside our glass-walled isolation booth, we will ask you our first question."

Jenny walked into the isolation booth, and an assistant fitted the earphones over her ears. Then the door was shut. She felt like something in a museum with everyone staring at her that way. Jenny carefully slipped the earphone off her left ear so as not to interfere with her special thought hearing.

"Here is the first question," Mr. Groper announced. "Who were the six wives of Henry the

Eighth? Give their names in the proper order, and tell what happened to each one."

"Catherine of Aragon was first," Jenny said. "And she was divorced. Then came"—she paused and frowned a little—"Anne Boleyn, and she was beheaded, and Jane Seymour was next, and she died, and then"—here Jenny closed her eyes and wrinkled her forehead—"Anne of Cleves, and *she* was divorced, and Catherine Howard was beheaded, and the last was"—she chewed the end of her forefinger, and waited until Mr. Groper looked uneasy—"the last was Catherine Parr, and she was still alive when King Henry died."

"Well done!" Mr. Groper said. "There's your first one thousand dollars. Now here is the second question: How do we determine the dates for each of the following holidays: Mother's Day, Thanksgiving Day, Labor Day, General Election Day, Easter and Sadie Hawkins Day?"

Jenny could have answered that right away, but she waited for a few moments. "Mother's Day is always the second Sunday in May," she said, "and Thanksgiving Day is always the fourth Thursday in November. Labor Day"—she looked up at the ceiling for a while—"is the first Monday in September, and General Election Day is the first Tuesday after the first Monday in November, and it comes in years ending in zero, four, and eight in the even decades, and in years ending in two and six in the odd decades. And Easter is the first Sunday after the first paschal full moon after March twenty-first."

"And how about Sadie Hawkins Day?" Mr. Groper asked.

"Oh," Jenny said. "Sadie Hawkins Day?" She screwed up her face tightly. "Sadie Hawkins day . . . let me see . . . ah! It's the first Saturday after November 11."

"Perfect!" Mr. Groper exclaimed, and the whole audience sighed with relief. Things were turning out much better than he had expected. Perhaps it would be all right after all.

"Now that's two thousand dollars," Mr. Groper said, rubbing his hands together. "You're doing very well, Jenny. Now for the third question. This one is about birds, and it's a hard one, and it has several parts. What state has the sea gull for its unofficial state bird?"

"Utah," Jenny said.

"And what state has a chicken for its bird?"

"Rhode Island."

"Good so far. Now try this. What states have the mocking bird for their official state bird?"

"Mocking bird?" Jenny repeated, as if she were surprised. "Well, Mississippi is one. And Tennessee. And . . . er . . . Texas." Then she frowned and drew her finger down the glass of her isolation booth. "And Florida."

"Is that all?" Mr. Groper asked.

"I think there's another one," Jenny said doubtfully, although she could hear the name as plain as anything in her left ear. She closed her eyes up tight and pressed her finger against her forehead. She squirmed and twisted and gave a despairing look out over the audience. Every one in the audience looked so unhappy that Jenny took pity on them and brightened up. "I think I know," she said. "Arkansas."

"Right!" Mr. Groper shouted, and the audience clapped loudly in relief.

He went on through all seventeen questions, ending up with a frightful one about the Federal Income Tax Schedule for a single person not qualifying as the head of a household. The questions had all been easy enough for Jenny to answer, but it took a lot of effort to make it look hard, and by the end of the

182

show she was tired. The audience clapped and clapped, and Mr. Groper congratulated her, but she was too sleepy to care. When they got back to the Ambassador Hotel she crawled into her bed, and the rest of the family came in to say good night to her.

"You were wonderful, Jenny," Joe said. "You did everything just right. That's seventeen thousand dollars you've earned already."

"Are you still feeling all right?" Stanley wondered. "Your ear still OK?"

Her father patted her on the shoulder. "Seventeen thousand," he muttered. "That's more than I can make in three years, and you did it in just one night. You're quite a girl, Jenny."

Her mother just kissed her and pulled up the covers, and Jenny was asleep almost as soon as they left the room.

The next Friday was the sixth of March, and everything went about the same as before. They had the same rooms at the Ambassador Hotel, and Mr. Groper shook hands with Jenny again, but this time his thoughts were much less gloomy about having kids on an adult show.

The questions were not much harder than before, but Jenny managed to make them look painful.

The last question was about the wives and families of the Presidents.

"Can you name," Mr. Groper said, "the one President who never married?"

Jenny nodded inside her glass isolation booth. "James Buchanan."

"Right," Mr. Groper said cheerily. "And who were the Presidents who had no children?"

"Washington was one," Jenny said. "And then there was Madison—and Polk. And Harding. And Buchanan. And I think one more." She went into another painful spell of concentration. "Could it be Andrew Jackson?"

"No, you mustn't ask," Mr. Groper said. "You must say definitely what you think is the answer."

"All right," Jenny said, "Andrew Jackson."

"Good!" Mr. Groper cried out joyfully. "And which President had the *most* children, Jenny?"

Jenny appeared to think this over. "John Tyler," she said after a while. "He had sixteen children in all."

"Wonderful!" Mr. Groper exclaimed, and the whole audience burst into a storm of clapping. Jenny smiled modestly.

"Congratulations, Jenny," Mr. Groper said. "That earns you a total so far of thirty-four thousand dollars. Now next Friday, if you can answer sixteen more questions, you can take a try at the grand final question, which can double your earnings and win you the hundred thousand dollars Grand Prize. And so we'll say good-by until next week, for our sponsors, the Hopper and Leach Soap Company, makers of Drift, Weft, Sift, Soothe, Sloth, Froth, Spume, and the new miracle Scud. Remember, when you think of soap, think of Hopper and Leach."

"I think Jenny looks tired," Mrs. Pearson said at supper the following Thursday. "These weekly trips to New York are wearing her out. And all the visitors! That photographer from *Life* was here all afternoon yesterday. And the night before the woman from *Hygeia* kept Jenny up until after ten o'clock. And before that it was *Parents' Magazine* and *Woman's Day*, and I don't know what else. I don't know if she ought to go to New York to-morrow."

"But Mom!" Stanley protested, "We can't take Jenny out of the 'Beat Your Brains' show *now!* Think of the millions of people who are *expecting* her. You can't disappoint them."

"I think I could," Mrs. Pearson said calmly, "if it was a question of Jenny's health. She's beginning to look quite pale, and all the excitement and publicity aren't good for her."

"There's just one more show," Joe said. "Then it will all be over, and things will calm down, and Jenny can get rested. And this is the show that will win us the Grand Prize, and then we can buy the hill. It's *very* important, you see."

"Not any more important than Jenny's health," his mother said. "How do you feel, Jenny?"

"All right. But I've *got* to go anyway, no matter how I feel. If I didn't, we'd lose the hill and the brook, and then I'd feel *terrible*. You see, it all depends on me. So I can't give up."

Mrs. Pearson spread out her hands in despair. "Well, I'm sure I don't know what to say. What do you think about it, Ed?"

Mr. Pearson took a long look at Jenny while he filled his pipe. "Well, I'm coming to think that the most important things for Jenny's health are the hill and the brook. I think perhaps we'd better let her go."

The next day was Friday, March 13. It was a bright day, and the snow was melting in the fields along the railroad, leaving big patches of brown earth or pressed-down grass.

186

At the studio Mr. Groper welcomed Jenny with open arms. "Ah, Jenny," he said, "you're *terrific*. According to the Trendex ratings *everybody* in the United States watches 'Beat Your Brains,' and all the other Friday evening shows are folding up, because nobody looks at them. We've reached the top, and we couldn't have done it without you."

"Thank you," Jenny said.

"And we certainly wish you luck," Mr. Groper went on. "The research experts say the questions for tonight are really hard. You look a little pale this evening. Are you worried about them?"

Jenny shook her head. "Not worried, just sort of tired, I guess."

Mr. Groper patted her gently on the shoulder. "I know what you mean, Jenny. It's a tough life being a performer. But the show must go on, you know, so keep your chin up."

The first question on this evening was about time. "When it's twelve o'clock noon in New York City," Mr. Groper asked, "what time is it in the following places? First, Boise, Idaho."

"Ten o'clock in the morning," Jenny said.

"Portland, Oregon?"

"Nine o'clock in the morning."

"Houston, Texas?"

"Eleven o'clock in the morning."

"London, England?"

Jenny did some counting on her fingers. "Five o'clock in the evening."

"And what time would it be in Athens, Greece?"

"Athens," Jenny repeated. "Seven o'clock in the evening."

"Right," said Mr. Groper. "And finally, what time would it be in Singapore?"

Jenny drew an imaginary globe with her finger on the glass wall of the isolation booth and began counting invisible zones across it. She frowned and began again. Finally she lifted her head and said slowly, "Twelve-thirty the next morning."

"Correct!" Mr. Groper chanted, "That's thirty-five thousand dollars now." He drew the next question card.

The show went on and on. There were questions about the kings of France, about the planets and their satellites, about various breeds of hunting dogs, about the formula for the speed of falling objects, and the sources of the world's principal rivers. Jenny grew more and more tired. She had short dizzy spells, and sometimes could scarcely hear what Mr. Groper was thinking. Her knees were wobbly, and she wanted to lie down and go to sleep. Once she was too dizzy to hear one of the questions, but she managed to recover in time to give the right answer, which was Leo, Virgo and Libra. She never did know what the question was.

Finally Mr. Groper came to the sixteenth question. "Can you name," he said, "three women in Shakespeare's plays who dressed as men?"

Jenny put her hands against the glass walls to steady herself. "Rosalind, in *As You Like It*," she murmured. "And . . . Viola, in *Twelfth Night*." The sounds in her left ear were much fainter. She had to listen hard to make out the words. "And Portia, in *The Merchant of Venice*."

"Good," Mr. Groper said encouragingly. "And the second part of that question is to name three male characters in literature who dressed as women."

Jenny turned her head and strained to listen. "Achilles," she said, "and . . . Toad, in . . . *The Wind in the Willows*, and"—she could feel her knees beginning to sag, and she straightened them up with an effort—"and Huckleberry Finn."

"Right!" Mr. Groper called out. "Wonderful work, Jenny! That earns you the sum of fifty thousand dollars. Now you have the chance of trying the Grand Final Question, and if you get that right, you can double your winnings and make it one hundred thousand dollars in all. Do you want to try it?"

Jenny nodded weakly.

Mr. Groper noticed how weak and pale she looked. "Would you like to have a little rest, Jenny?" he asked. "We can give you a short break to let you collect your thoughts."

Jenny shook her head quickly. The thoughts had been coming in fainter and fainter, and she was sure if she waited much longer, she wouldn't be able to hear them at all. They would have to hurry.

"All right," Mr. Groper said. "Then here is the Grand Final Question. If you can answer it correctly, you win the top prize of one hundred thousand dollars. If you can't answer it, you keep the fifty thousand dollars you have already won, and the wonderful record of answering fifty very difficult questions without a single mistake. Are you ready?"

Jenny nodded, but she could feel herself swaying and had to put up her hands against the glass walls. Her eyes kept closing no matter how hard she tried to keep them open.

"Here it is," Mr. Groper said, looking at his card. "Can you name *nine* memorable events that took place on April 18, and the years when they happened?"

"In 1775," Jenny said weakly, "Paul Revere's ride. On April 18, 1884, the steamships *Pomona* and *State of California* had a collision and one hundred fifty lives were lost . . . on April 18, 1906"—her head slumped down, but she forced herself to hold it up again—"there was the terrible San Francisco earthquake and fire, and on April 18, 1942, Lieutenant Colonel Doolittle . . . made his airplane raid over Tokyo . . . and on April 18, 1946, the . . . League of . . . Nations turned over its property to the . . . United Nations."

It was getting *very* hard to hear any thoughts, and she had to strain to catch the words. And her knees were going to buckle any minute, and if she fell down, she was sure she could never get up again, and she would lose her chance to save her brook and hill. She would *have* to stand up. She clenched her fists and went on.

"On April 18, 1949, Ireland cut its official ties with Britain, and on April 18, 1954, Gamel Abdel . . . Gamel Abdel . . . Nasser became premier of . . . of Egypt . . . and on April 18, 1955, Albert"—the whole studio was whirling around, and she *couldn't* keep her eyes open—"Albert Einstein died . . . and on

April 18, 1956 . . ." Her voice trailed away. She could feel a great black space rushing around and around her head. But she could hear words coming through the rushing sound. It was Mr. Groper's voice, encouraging her.

"The last question, Jenny. What happened on April 18, 1956?"

Jenny took a deep breath and held her hands tight against the glass walls. "Grace . . . Kelly . . . married Prince . . . Rainier . . . in Monaco." And then a wonderful soft darkness closed in on her and her knees suddenly bent, and she slumped down to the floor.

CHAPTER SIXTEEN

SHE opened her eyes cautiously.

"Good morning, Jenny," her mother said, looking at her anxiously. "How do you feel?"

"All right, Mommy. Is it time for school?"

"No, Jenny. This is Saturday. And besides, you're in New York."

"Oh," Jenny said. Then she sat up suddenly. "Did I win the Grand Prize?"

"You certainly did," Mr. Pearson said. "And we have the check right here in this envelope. We haven't opened it yet. You should be the one who opens it, because you won it."

Joe handed Jenny a letter opener from the table, and every one leaned over to watch while she cut open the envelope and pulled out a green check. It said *Pay to the order of* JENNY PEARSON *One hundred thousand and no/100* dollars, and it was signed with a great black scrawl that was supposed to be someone's name, but no one could read it.

"Think of that, Jenny!" Joe said. "A hundred thousand! Now we can buy the hill from Mr. Watson. Won't *he* be surprised! I can hardly wait to see his face."

"*I* can hardly wait to get this safely deposited in the Westfield bank," Mr. Pearson said. "It's a lot of money to have on one little piece of paper."

"You better keep it, Pop," Stanley suggested. "And we'll get Mom to sew up the pocket so it can't get out. Remember, New York is full of pickpockets."

"I was afraid something was going to go wrong yesterday," Joe said. "It was Friday the thirteenth, but I didn't want to say anything about it because it might make Jenny nervous or something."

"Why, that's right, it was the thirteenth," Mr. Pearson said. "Well, it's all safe in our hands now." He folded the check carefully and put it in his wallet. "I guess the bad luck passed us by that time."

"There's something else in this envelope," Stanley reported, pulling out a folded piece of paper. "It has something printed on it."

"Read it," Joe said.

"It's too long. Here, you look at it."

They all looked at it.

FEDERAL TAX LAWS

Every citizen or resident of the United States with a gross income of $600 or more must file an income tax report. Form 1040 is used by all whose income is $5,000 or over. All prizes won in radio and television contests, such as give-away programs, must be reported.

Recipients of prizes are urged to consult the enclosed Income Tax Rate Schedule before making plans to spend their prize money.

"Oh, *no!*" Joe said in alarm. "I didn't know we had to pay *taxes* on this."

"By jing, I forgot all about income taxes," Mr. Pearson said. "I was so surprised to see Jenny win all that money that I never thought of it as *income* at all. It was more like an accident."

"That's going to cut into our surplus, I guess," Stanley said, "But as long as we can still buy the hill from Mr. Watson, that's the main thing."

"Well, let's look at the schedule and see what the taxes will be," Joe said. He ran his finger down the column of figures. " 'Single Taxpayers who do not qualify as head of household.' That's Jenny, I guess. 'Over 100,000 dollars, but not over 150,000

196

dollars, the tax is 67,320 dollars, plus 89 per cent of excess over 100,000 dollars.' What does all that mean? 'The tax is 67,320 dollars.' *Good grief! Sixty-seven thousand!* Quick, where's a pencil?" He scribbled some figures down on the back of the paper and did a hasty subtraction.

"Why, that's going to leave only 32,680 dollars! That won't be anywhere *near* enough!"

"What a shame!" Mrs. Pearson said, putting her arms around Jenny, who buried her face in her mother's shoulder. "And after all that you children have done."

The ride home on the train that afternoon was a gloomy one. After the electric locomotive had been changed for a diesel at New Haven, Stanley brightened up a bit. "After all, we've got thirty-two thousand dollars. All we've got to do is to earn another forty thousand or so. By the way, Jenny, how's your ear this morning? Can you hear any thoughts?"

"I can hear what you're thinking," Jenny said wearily. "You want me to go on another quiz show."

"I'm afraid I can't allow that," Mrs. Pearson said. "Jenny's already had much too much of that."

Joe had been studying the tax rate schedule. "Besides, Stanley, suppose Jenny won another hundred thousand dollars. That would make her income two hundred thousand, and the tax on *that* is 156,820 dollars. That would leave us with 43,180 dollars, and that still wouldn't be enough. And if she won *another* hundred thousand, that would bring our total up to only 52,000 dollars, and even *that* wouldn't be enough."

"You mean if she won *three* hundred thousand dollars we *still* couldn't buy the hill?" Stanley was horrified. "Why, that's . . . why, it's . . . how can they *do* that to us?"

Mr. Pearson shrugged his shoulders. "Well, taxes are taxes. You have to pay them. That's just the way it is, that's all."

"When do we have to pay the taxes?" Stanley wanted to know.

"In April, a year from now," his father said.

"Well, why don't we just buy the hill from Mr. Watson now and try to get the money for taxes later on?" Stanley suggested.

"Oh, no we *don't*," Mr. Pearson said. "Other people have tried that, and it usually gets them in trouble with Uncle Sam."

"Wait a minute," Joe said, "there's something here about deductions. 'Total allowable deductions for contributions to churches, tax-exempt educational institutions and hospitals is 30 per cent of taxpayer's adjusted gross income.' That means we could give away—let's see—thirty thousand dollars to the Pearson's Corners church. That would be all right, wouldn't it, Pop?"

"I guess so, but you'd better break the news gently to the minister. He might not be able to stand the shock."

Stanley peered over Joe's shoulder. "If you gave away thirty thousand, how much would the taxes be?"

Joe looked down the column of figures. "Say—42,120 dollars. That would save us a lot of taxes! It was sixty-seven thousand before."

"Yes, but how much would we have *left?*" Stanley persisted.

Joe did some figuring. "Only 27,880 dollars. That's less than we had the other way. I guess *that* won't help much."

There was a gloomy silence all the way to Springfield, and there wasn't much conversation while they waited for the 4:53 for Westfield, and the nine miles to Westfield were pretty quiet too, and no one was feeling very happy when they drove home in the gray evening, especially when they turned up the hill out of Pearson's Corners and could see their old house against the evening sky and they all thought how different everything was going to be soon, when the hill was covered with houses and streets.

When they got into the house the telephone was ringing. The telephone-answering device had been unused since February, when the boys had become more interested in managing Jenny's quiz programs, so Stanley ran to answer it.

"Tarboro, North Carolina, calling Miss Jenny Pearson," the operator said.

"This is Jenny Pearson's manager," Stanley said. "I'll take the call for her."

"Hello?" a voice barked at him. "You're Miss Pearson's manager? Well, this is Willard Watmore, at Earl University. Head of the Parapsychology Laboratory here at Earl. Psychical research. Been trying to get you all afternoon. Saw Miss Pearson on television program last night. Extremely interesting case. Very anxious to interview her. Could fly up from Tarboro tomorrow. Appointment for tomorrow afternoon? Five o'clock?"

"Well...yes," Stanley said.

"Right. Good-by."

"Who was that, Stanley?" his mother said.

"Oh, it was somebody at Earl University. He's coming up tomorrow to interview Jenny about something."

Jenny sighed. *"Another* interview?"

"Oh, this is nothing to worry about," Stanley reassured her. "This is just a university, and they don't have any money to give away. Besides, we're in such a high tax bracket that we'd only get a little bit of it anyway."

Breakfast the next morning was not a very happy occasion. The television quiz had worked out so perfectly that it was hard to take the disappointment. Mr. and Mrs. Pearson kept trying to change the subject.

"The ice on the pond's beginning to melt," Mr. Pearson said, looking out the window.

"And that's probably the last ice we'll ever see there," Joe said.

"But the flowers will be up soon," Mr. Pearson said brightly. "Just think, it's March fifteenth already."

"Just one month to go before the bulldozers start in," Stanley added.

Jenny just sighed and looked down at her plate. She didn't have the heart to finish her oatmeal.

That evening at six minutes past five a yellow taxi from Westfield drove into their driveway. A short, squarish sort of man got out and walked briskly up to their door. Stanley was expecting him and opened the door just as the man was reaching for the knocker.

"Pearson?" the man asked.

Stanley nodded. "Come in, Mr.—"

"Watmore," the man said. "Willard Watmore."

Mrs. Pearson hurried out from the kitchen and invited Mr. Watmore into the living room. Jenny was lying on the floor looking at her pictures in *Life* magazine. She got up when Mr. Watmore came in.

He bowed stiffly from the waist and shook her hand. "Miss Pearson, I'm Professor Watmore, of the Parapsychology Laboratory at Earl University. Research in extrasensory perception. Difficult science. Hard to find suitable subjects for investigation. Saw you on 'Beat Your Brains' program on television. Remarkable performance, but suspected right away it was not memory but telepathic communication."

Jenny raised her eyebrows at this.

"That is," Professor Watmore explained, "I suspected you were getting your answers from someone else's thoughts and not from your own memory. Am I right?"

Jenny looked over at Joe and Stanley to see what

she should say to this question, but they merely shrugged their shoulders. After all, the quiz program was over, and there was no use in keeping it a secret any longer.

Jenny looked down at the floor. "Yes," she said in a low voice. "I could hear what the quizmaster was thinking, and that's how I could answer all the questions."

Professor Watmore looked at her and smiled. "But don't be *ashamed* of it! You have a remarkable gift, young lady. A lot more remarkable than being able to remember who invented the doorknob, or some silly thing like that. Your television people didn't know it, but they were demonstrating something far more wonderful than a good memory. Your mind is more than just a collection of bits of information. Your mind can *do* things. And I would like to find out what it can do. May I give you a few simple tests? Just a few minutes. Nothing difficult."

Jenny nodded.

"Is that all right, Mrs. Pearson?" the professor asked.

"Yes, but I hope you won't tire her out. She's had too much excitement these last three weeks."

"Shouldn't wonder," Professor Watmore said. "I'll be careful. Now, Miss Pearson, if you will sit down here at the table." He took a small package from his pocket. "This is a routine test we give to all subjects. I have a deck of cards here. There are five different designs on them—a star, a circle, a cross, a square, and waves. There are five cards of each design. Twenty-five cards in all. If you will try to guess the design on each card before I turn it up, we'll see how many you can guess right. Do you understand?"

"Yes," Jenny said. The others gathered around the table to watch. They went through the pack, but Jenny had only three right.

"I didn't do very well, did I?" she said.

"Oh, that doesn't matter," the professor said. "I'm just trying to find out what sort of perception you have. That first test was for clairvoyance, to see if you could know the next card without seeing it. The next test is for precognition."

"What's that?" Jenny said.

"That's the ability to know about something *before* it happens. Now you write down the order you think the cards are going to be in after I've shuffled them. Here's a paper and pencil."

They tried that, but Jenny didn't do any better than before.

"That's all right," the professor reassured her. "Now for psychokinesis."

"For *what?*" Jenny asked, drawing back a little.

"That's making things happen simply by thinking about them. We call it PK. Here are some dice. See if you can roll a certain number. What number would you like?"

"One," Jenny said.

"All right, try to roll ones," the professor said.

Jenny rolled the dice about twenty times, but ones came up only twice. Then the professor rolled the dice while Jenny thought hard about ones, but that was no better.

Professor Watmore seemed pleased. "Fine," he said. "Our tests have ruled out clairvoyance, precognition and PK. Now let's try telepathy. That's sensing something in another person's mind. If I'm not mistaken, that's what you have a special gift for. I'm going to take the cards and sit over here." He walked across the room and sat down in the leather armchair in the corner. "Now I'll turn up the cards one by one, and I'll look at them, and you try to tell me what design is on each one." He looked at the first card. "What's on this one?"

"Waves," Jenny said.

Professor Watmore nodded and looked at the next card. "And on this one?"

"A star."

He nodded again and went on through the whole pack, and Jenny was right on every one. The professor was *very* pleased at that, and then he went into the kitchen and called out from there, to see if Jenny could sense his thoughts from that distance. Of course Jenny's family knew she could do that, so it wasn't very exciting to watch. But it seemed to excite the professor. He came bouncing back into the room with a big smile. "That's it! An amazing case of *pure* telepathy. In all my career I've never seen such a *perfect* telepathic subject. The Society for Psychical Research is going to go wild when they hear of it. Just think, for seventy-five years they have been looking for a subject like this, and finally they've found one. Professor Bidworth will be delighted! I can hardly *wait* to get back to tell them."

Professor Watmore darted about the room, picking up his dice and cards and papers. Finally he located his hat, but Mrs. Pearson asked him to stay for supper. He hesitated. "But what about the cab driver? He's been out there for more than an hour already."

"Well, he can have supper with us too," Mrs. Pearson said.

Just then the kitchen door opened and Mr. Pearson came in with the cab driver. "Do you know who I found sitting out in the taxi outside?" he said. "It's Ernie Kubashev! Oh, how do you do?" Mr. Pearson said, noticing Professor Watmore.

"Professor Watmore is going to stay for supper," Mrs. Pearson said, "and we hope Ernie will eat with us too."

"Sure he will," Mr. Pearson said. "Won't you, Ernie?"

Ernie scratched his head. "Well, I guess I can if my fare is going to stay for supper. There's nothing in the taxi company rules that says I shouldn't."

"You see," Mr. Pearson said, after they were well launched into the baked beans, "Ernie's father has a farm up the valley about two miles, and Ernie used to come up here in the winter to go sliding when he was little. Then he took up skiing when he was in high school and got to be a junior state champion. And he learned to ski right on our hill here. We're proud of him. Did you get a chance to ski at all this winter, Ernie?"

"Well, that taxi keeps me pretty busy, Mr. Pearson, but I drove a bus up to Pittsfield for the Westfield High Ski Club, and I just happened to have my skiis along, and so I managed to get in a few runs. Say, I hear that Mr. Watson's going to sell off his property for house lots. Does that mean the hill too?"

Mr. Pearson nodded and tried to change the subject. "Have some more beans, Ernie? Professor Watmore?"

"That's a shame," Ernie went on. "That hill is the best natural ski hill that I've seen anywhere. No rocks, and it keeps its snow beautifully. An awful lot of kids could have a good time on that hill."

"Have another biscuit, Ernie," Mrs. Pearson urged him. "And . . . and how are your mother and father these days?"

"Oh, they're fine, Mrs. Pearson, but isn't there some way to get Mr. Watson to leave the hill the way it is? Perhaps the town could buy it from him."

"Not at *his* price," Mr. Pearson said. "The town doesn't have seventy-five thousand dollars to spend."

"Excuse me," Professor Watmore said, "but is this the hill that Miss Pearson spoke of on the television program? The one that she wanted to buy?"

"That's right," Mr. Pearson told him.

"And the prize money wasn't enough?"

"Not after taxes had taken two thirds of it."

"I see," the professor said. "Are there chances for other TV programs?"

"That wouldn't help much," Joe told him. "Jenny's in the 90 per cent tax bracket now, so she can keep only 10 per cent of what she makes."

"And there's only a few weeks to go before the bulldozers move in and start tearing the place up," Stanley added.

"That poses a difficult problem," the professor said, resting his chin in his hand. "But there may be an answer to it."

The children all looked intently at him.

"Grants of money for research purposes are tax-exempt," he mused, "but I don't suppose anyone in this family is a candidate for a degree in psychology."

"Not as far as I know," Mr. Pearson said.

"Besides," the professor went on, "you need more than forty thousand dollars, and that's a whopping research grant. What you need is to have someone buy the hill *for* you. In that way you won't have to pay taxes on any more income."

Stanley brightened up at this. "That's a *good* idea. Who do you think would buy it for us?"

The professor rubbed his chin and frowned. "Well, I don't know. But I think there might be someone who would be so interested in telepathy that he would put up the money. I'll have to think about it for a while. Perhaps someone in the Society for Psychical Research. Well, I'll let you know if I think of something." He looked at his watch. "My, it's almost eight o'clock! I'll have to hurry. A *most* successful interview, Mr. and Mrs. Pearson. Your daughter has a remarkable psychic faculty. A wonderful subject for research. Would you mind if a few of my colleagues dropped in from time to time to conduct a few experiments?"

"Well," Mr. Pearson said, "we feel that Jenny's had a little too much excitement lately, and we'd like to have her get some rest for a while."

"Oh, we would be very careful," the professor assured him. "We are interested in her health too, you see. And in the meanwhile, I'll be looking around for someone to help you out with this hill."

Mr. Pearson looked at his wife. "I guess it would be all right, if there won't be too much excitement."

"Thank you, sir," Professor Watmore said, shaking Mr. Pearson's hand. "And thank you for the delicious dinner, Mrs. Pearson. And thank *you*, Jenny, for your help. Take care of yourself, for psychic research *needs* you." He shook hands all around, gathered up his hat and hurried out the door.

CHAPTER SEVENTEEN

ON THURSDAY there was a telegram.

HAVE ELDERLY LADY INTERESTED TELEP-
ATHY WANTS APPOINTMENT FRIDAY PM.
SIGNED WATMORE.

"Good," Stanley said. "That's what we're looking for. Tell him to send her along."

The elderly lady turned out to be a Mrs. Cooperthwaite from Philadelphia, and she wanted Jenny to get in touch with the spirit personality of her husband, who had died twenty-five years before. Jenny couldn't hear a sound from the spirit personality, and Mrs. Cooperthwaite was very disappointed. She gave Jenny a one-dollar bill for trying.

An advertising man came on the following Tuesday. He was a fast-talking man in a gray suit, and he wanted to use Jenny's telepathy to find out what sort of things people really wanted to buy. "You see," he said, "advertising is different from what it used to be. In the old days you simply tried to get people to buy your product, but nobody believes what the ads say any more, so we have to go out and find what people want, so the manufacturer can make it. But you can't believe what people say. They say they want big cars, but then they buy small ones. They say they wouldn't be caught dead in a chemise dress, but they all buy chemise dresses. You see? It isn't what they *say* that counts. You've got to find out what they *think*. That's where your sister comes in."

But they found out that he didn't have the slightest interest in buying Mr. Watson's hill for them. Or any hill for that matter. And so he left, and they glumly watched his car going down the road into Pearson's Corners. Things weren't working out so well.

On Sunday evening—that was the twenty-ninth of March—Mr. Hagerty dropped in. He said he had something he wanted to talk to the family about, so they got him comfortably settled in the living room, and Stanley brought him a box of matches so he could light his pipe. He didn't say much until he got the pipe going, but after that he leaned back in the chair and began.

"You know that TV show that your Jenny was on in New York? Well, I heard what she said about trying to buy this hill from Mr. Watson so it wouldn't be all built up with houses. Well, we were all pleased that she won the contest, and then we were sorry that taxes wouldn't leave enough to pay Watson's price for the hill. But I didn't think much more about it for a while, until I heard the school kids talking about it the other day, and they were saying it was too bad they weren't going to have that hill to slide on any more, and I told them that they shouldn't feel too bad, because it would bring a lot of money into Pearson's Corners—you know, with more houses and people and children all needing things from the stores. But then my little girl asked me what all the new children were going to do if we turned everything into house lots. Where was there going to be any place to slide? Well, I thought that over, and I began to think she had a point there. So I talked to some of the other selectmen, and some of them had begun to think about the same thing. So today we went up to the Watsons' after church and talked things over with him."

The Pearsons all leaned forward at this. "What did he say?" Mr. Pearson said.

Mr. Hagerty frowned. "He said quite a lot. Said the country was getting bigger, and we were just standing in the way of progress. Said the cities were overcrowded, and it was the duty of the towns to take in people who wanted to move out of cities. Everything's getting bigger these days, he said, and we just have to move along with the tide. He said we ought to be patriotic like him, and welcome the extra population into the town."

"And what did you say?" Mr. Pearson wanted to know.

"We told him that it was fine to be patriotic, but he ought to think of his own town too. And then we said that there would be a lot of people in Pearson's Corners who would sell some land to people who want to move out of the city, and if he would give his hill to the town, we would guarantee to sell the same amount of land to city folks. In that way we could sort of spread the patriotism around over the town, and not have a whole lot of houses all jammed together in one place, *and* the kids could still have a hill to slide on."

"And what did he think of that?" Mr. Pearson said.

Mr. Hagerty scratched the back of his neck. "He didn't think much of it. In fact, he got kind of sore and said we were trying to cheat him out of the profits he deserved for having a little foresight and initiative. He said if he did what we suggested, *we'd* all be making money, and he'd be losing it. He said that it was a man's patriotic duty to stand up for his rights, and he knew what *his* rights were. After that we figured we'd gone about as far as we could on that tack, so we got up and went home. I'm sorry we couldn't do any better. I just thought I'd drop in and tell you about it. We wanted you to know that the town's all behind your kids and you on this thing, but we don't have the money to pay Watson's price."

"I know," Mr. Pearson said. "The town couldn't do that. And thanks for trying to help. I guess there's not much we can do about it now."

Mr. Hagerty shook his head. "Nope, I guess not. Well, so long, Ed. G'night, Mrs. Pearson. Good night, kids." He thumped Joe and Stanley on their backs and ran his big hand through Jenny's hair, and then he went out the door.

The next Tuesday was the last day of March, and that evening there was another telegram from Professor Watmore.

FBI INTERESTED TELEPATHY WANT JENNY ON TRIAL APRIL 6 EXPERIMENT SIGNED WATMORE

"The FBI!" Stanley said. "Now we're *really* getting somewhere. If we can get the Federal government interested, we'll be all set. They could buy the whole town if they wanted to."

"*If* they wanted to," Joe reminded him. "And anyhow, the telegram said they only wanted Jenny on trial, so they just want to try her out for a while before they decide to use her. Who knows how long that will take? And there's only two more weeks to April 15."

On Saturday a tall young man came to see them. He said his name was Bailey, and he worked for the Federal Bureau of Investigation. He explained that the bureau had been interested for some time in the idea of using telepathy as a means of investigation, and the Parapsychology Laboratory at Earl University had recommended Jenny as having the strongest extrasensory perception in the country. "What we want to do," Mr. Bailey said, "is to have your daughter sit in on a trial and listen to the defendant's thoughts, and then her testimony can be used as evidence. You see, law enforcement has one great handicap, and that is that you can't find out what people are actually *thinking*. The old galvanometers—you know, the lie detectors—aren't very dependable, and besides, they only show whether a person is lying or not. With a really good

217

mind reader, we can get right at the *thoughts* of a person, and that ought to make our job a lot simpler."

Mr. Pearson looked puzzled. "But is this right—I mean, is it legal to do that?"

Mr. Bailey looked at him and smiled. "Do you think we'd be doing it if it wasn't legal, Mr. Pearson?"

"Well . . . no, I suppose not, but—"

"But Mr. Bailey," Mrs. Pearson said, "do you think it's good to have this young girl sit in court and listen to the thoughts of *criminals?* As her mother, I don't see how I could allow that to go on."

"Oh, I understand your concern, ma'am," Mr. Bailey said, "but we wouldn't think of having your daughter sit in on trials for homicide or anything like that. As a matter of fact, the case that we had in mind to experiment with was a mail fraud case. You see, there is this druggist up in Skowhegan, Maine, who goes by the name of Doc Pulsifer, and he's developed what he calls a 'Fish Whistle.' It has a long plastic tube and you put the whistle end down in the water and you blow on the other end and it's supposed to call fish so you can catch them. And he's been sending out advertising matter in the mails, and a man in Ipswich bought one and didn't

218

catch any fish and complained to the Post Office Department and they took the matter to court. The Federal court is going to take it up on April 6 in Boston."

"In Boston?" Mrs. Pearson said. "Would Jenny have to go all that way?"

Mr. Bailey smiled. "It's less than two hours along the turnpike, ma'am. We would leave here at eight-thirty in the morning, and have her back here by five." He glanced at Joe and Stanley. "And we'd like to take along these two boys, ma'am, if you can spare them. They'd be some company for the girl, and it would be an interesting experience for them."

"*Can* we, Mom?" both boys said at once.

"But what about school?" Mrs. Pearson said. "You've been away so much this winter. Mr. Billings wouldn't like it."

"I think we can fix it up with the school principal, ma'am," Mr. Bailey said. "I'll stop in and explain it to him. I don't think he'll object."

Mrs. Pearson hesitated. "It's asking a lot to have you keep an eye on those three children like that. Won't that be too much for you?"

"I think we can handle it, ma'am. We're used to keeping an eye on people."

"And I suppose it will be quite safe?"

"Oh, *Mother!*" Stanley protested. "There's nothing safer than the FBI."

"Well," Mrs. Pearson said, "I'll call up your father and ask him what he thinks."

She came back in a moment. "He says it sounds all right to him. And he said maybe they would want to have a pair of handcuffs to keep Stanley from getting lost."

Stanley blushed, and Mr. Bailey laughed. "All right then. We'll be here at eight-thirty Monday morning, and I'll have the handcuffs." He winked at Stanley and picked up his gray felt hat. "Well, good-by, ma'am. Good-by, kids. Monday morning at eight-thirty."

As soon as he was gone, Joe and Stanley let out a whoop and started wrestling together on the floor. When they rolled into the table leg the lamp would have toppled off, if Mrs. Pearson hadn't caught it.

"My, my," she said with a sigh. "Things used to be simpler before all this *listening* began."

On Monday Mr. Bailey arrived in a black car, and he had another man with him. "This is Mr. Bergamini, kids," Mr. Bailey said. "He's got the handcuffs for Stanley. Had your breakfast? Let's go."

The children all got into the back seat and waved good-by to their mother as they rolled down the hill in the black car. They slipped through the center of Pearson's Corners, past the Town Hall and the Congregational church and Pearson's Hardware, and in no time they had reached the Massachusetts Turnpike, and were streaking away toward Boston. It was a sunny day, and even though it was only the sixth of April, the willows beside the brooks and ponds were turning yellow along their drooping branches, and there were green patches in the fields where the ground was wet. Mr. Bergamini was driving, with his left shoulder hunched up against the car door, and his eyes never moving from the road ahead. Stanley was watching the speedometer, and he nudged Joe with his elbow.

"Seventy," he whispered, and Joe nodded.

"When are you going to ask him about buying the hill?" Jenny said in Joe's ear.

"Mr. Bailey," Joe said, "do you think the Federal government would buy a hill for us if Jenny's telepathy works out all right?"

"Perhaps. Let's see now, you want to buy that hill from a Mr. Henry Watson, and he's asking seventy-five thousand dollars, and you won one hundred thousand on a TV show, of which taxes will take over sixty-seven thousand, leaving you with thirty-two thousand. The selectmen have asked Mr. Watson to give the hill to the town for a playground, but he said no. He is going to sell his house in Pearson's Corners and move to Florida before November."

"Gosh," Joe said. "How did you know all that?"

"We make it our business to know things," Mr. Bailey said. "You'd be surprised how much we know. The only trouble is, we haven't been able to find out what people are *thinking*. That's why we're so interested in Jenny. Telepathy may be the answer to our problem. We'll try her out on a few cases, and if it works out all right, the bureau's going to feel pretty good about it, and they might see their way to buying up that hill for you."

"Wonderful!" Stanley said. "That's awful generous of the FBI to do that."

"Well, it isn't all generosity," Mr. Bailey said. "We consulted the Parapsychology Laboratory at Earl University, and they told us that a big disappointment like losing that hill might disturb Jenny's telepathy, and we wouldn't want that to happen. If this case works out today, we'll see if something can't be done about the hill."

"Oh, *good*," Jenny breathed happily. "But there's

not much time left. The bulldozers are coming in soon."

"April 16," Mr. Bailey said. "We know that too."

They drove into the center of Boston along Huntington Avenue. "You kids ever been in Boston before?" Mr. Bailey asked them. "No? Well, this big park is Boston Common. That's where the British redcoats used to drill back in 1775. And over there to the left is the Charles River, where Paul Revere rowed across to Charlestown to begin his ride out to Lexington and Concord. You know about Paul Revere's ride, don't you?"

"Sure," Stanley said. "He was going out to warn the Minute Men. One if by land and two if by sea."

"Miss Romaine's been to Concord," Jenny said. "She has a picture of Walden Pond in our classroom. There was somebody important that built a cabin there. I can't remember what his name was."

"Henry Thoreau," Mr. Bailey said. "He built his cabin in 1845. He was a queer duck, that Thoreau. He said he'd rather follow his conscience than the law."

"Miss Romaine said the cabin's not there any more," Jenny added. "There's just a heap of stones that people have piled up where the cabin was."

When they reached the Federal Court Building Mr. Bailey led them upstairs and through a door that said *United States District Court* in gold letters. They were in a big room with a high desk on one side and solid-looking tables and dark curtains on the windows. Mr. Bailey motioned to them to sit down at one of the tables.

Pretty soon a short man in a brown suit came in and sat down at another table. His face was round and sunburned, as if he had been outdoors a lot, and his hair was gray and he had a bald spot on the top of his head. He leaned back in his chair and smiled at the children. He had bushy eyebrows.

"That's Doc Pulsifer," Mr. Bailey said in a low voice. "He's the man who makes the Fish Whistle."

Just then a man came in wearing a long black robe and he sat down behind the high desk, and some more men came in with briefcases and sat down at the tables. A man in a black suit stood up and announced in a loud voice, "The United States District Court is now in session. The case of United States versus Orin Pulsifer."

The men with the briefcases took turns standing up and talking about "fraudulent intent" and "*malo animo*," and Mr. Bailey whispered that they were the lawyers and the man in the black robe was the

225

judge. The lawyers liked to speak in very long words, and sometimes in Latin, and the three children were having a hard time keeping track of the argument, but finally one of the lawyers stood up and announced that the government had a special witness. "Because of this person's unusual ability to read the thoughts of other people," the lawyer said, "she should be able to give some evidence of the actual intent of the defendant in regard to his product and his own opinion of it."

Mr. Bailey nudged Jenny and told her to stand up. The lawyer introduced her to the judge, and he leaned over the edge of the high desk and peered at her over the rims of his glasses. "I've heard of you before, young lady," he said, "and I understand that you have a most remarkable talent."

Jenny didn't know what to say to this, so she smiled faintly and didn't say anything. Then the lawyer said that he was going to ask Mr. Pulsifer a question, and he wanted Jenny to listen very carefully to what Mr. Pulsifer was thinking and then report it to the court. "And please be sure to report his thoughts exactly as you hear them," he said. "Don't change a single word."

"All right," the lawyer said. "Mr. Pulsifer, we want you to think about this question: What chance does anyone have of catching a fish when using your Fish Whistle?"

Jenny listened. The courtroom was perfectly quiet and everybody looked at her. At first she didn't hear anything at all, and a frown passed over her face. When she finally did hear something, she was surprised how faint it was. Doc Pulsifer must be a very quiet thinker, she thought.

"Well," the lawyer said at last, "did you hear anything?"

"Yes," Jenny said. "What I heard was 'You can always catch suckers if you fish deep enough.' That's all there was."

"There!" the lawyer said, turning to the judge behind the high desk. "*That* ought to be evidence enough of the intent of the defendant. His motives were obviously to deceive the unsuspecting public, whom he likes to think of as 'suckers.'"

The judge peered down from his high desk at Jenny and then at Doc Pulsifer. After a while he folded his hands and nodded. The man in the black suit rapped once on his desk with a wooden mallet. The lawyers all stopped talking among themselves and looked up at the judge.

The judge was short and had a round pink face, and a wisp of his white hair came down over his forehead. Jenny noticed that when he spoke, his cheeks puffed in and out. "In the light of the evidence just produced," the judge said, "it is the opinion of this court that the defendant is guilty of using the United States mails to defraud the public. Therefore, pursuant to an Act of Congress of September 19, 1890, we request the Postmaster General to forbid the use of the mails for distribution of any literature pertaining to the defendant's Fish Whistle. We would like to express the appreciation of this court to the young lady"—and here he looked down at Jenny—"for her help in what might have been a very difficult case. And now has the defendant any remarks to make before we adjourn the court?"

Doc Pulsifer got up slowly and stood with his weather-tanned hands on the back of his chair. "Your Honor, I would like to say just a few words. I've got to hand it to that little girl for her mind reading. She said exactly what I was thinking. The only trouble is that you folks didn't understand what I meant. What I meant was that you can always catch *some* kind of fish if you know how to go about it. And a sucker is a well-known American fish. Not much of a fish for fighting, of course, but they're good eating in the spring, and you can take

them with a worm most anytime in April and in May, so long as the water runs good and cold. But what I mean to say is, you folks got me all wrong about this sucker business, because down where I come from a sucker is a *fish,* but here in Boston—and in other cities too, I shouldn't wonder—I guess you think a sucker is a human being."

The judge raised his white eyebrows but he didn't say anything.

Doc Pulsifer took a deep breath. "Now that's all I want to say about fish, but I've got something else that's got to be said before you adjourn this court, and that is that this case wasn't a proper case, and I'll tell you why. When you go to poke around in a man's mind, and to take his thoughts out of his head without his say-so, you're doing something that isn't right. And not only it isn't right, but it's plumb against the Constitution, where it says that the right of the people to be secure in their persons against unreasonable searches shall not be violated. And the Constitution also says that private property shall not be taken for public use without just compensation. And where I come from we hold that a man's thoughts are his private property, and I don't recollect that anybody in this court compensated me for my thought, and it was a pretty average good thought too. Not that I blame this little girl here, 'cause she was just doing what she was told and probably didn't know any better. But I want to tell this court that the way I look at it they have accepted evidence here that is contrary to the Constitution, and I'm going to appeal this case and even take it to the Supreme Court if I have to, and we'll see what *they've* got to say about it."

Jenny blushed when Doc Pulsifer said she didn't know any better and she could feel the warmth creep over her face. Her ears grew hot, and there was a faint ringing sound, as when you hear a loud noise.

The judge frowned and looked gravely over his glasses. The bailiff banged his mallet on his desk, and Mr. Bailey led the children out of the room. He looked pretty disappointed. "That queers the whole thing," he said. "Well, let's go get some lunch, anyway."

They found a restaurant down the street, and they all had lamb chops and mashed potatoes and peas, and Joe and Stanley had banana splits for dessert. "It's only one-thirty," Mr. Bailey said. "We still have an hour to kill. What do you say we go over to the Navy Yard in Charlestown and take a look at *Old Ironsides?*"

They hunted up Mr. Bergamini and the car, and he drove them over a high bridge to the shipyard. They could see the tall masts of *Old Ironsides* long before they reached the pier. Mr. Bailey took them aboard, and they went all over the ship. Everything was neat and shining with varnish and new paint, and the brass gleamed in the sunlight, especially the great ship's bell with U.S.S. CONSTITUTION on it.

"Gee," Stanley said in admiration, "they really keep it in shape, don't they? Do you think it could still sail?"

A sailor was polishing the brass mountings of the ship's bell, and he looked at Stanley and smiled. "She sure could, kid. The old lady's just as seaworthy as ever, and don't let them tell you anything different."

An officer walked up and rang the bell five times.

"Half past two," Mr. Bailey said. "Time to go, or we'll never make it. I promised your mother I'd have you back by five o'clock, and we've got all that Boston traffic."

On the way home Mr. Bailey was pretty quiet, and the children could see that things hadn't gone as well as he had hoped. Finally Joe asked the question they all had in their minds.

"Mr. Bailey, what are the chances now for having the FBI buy that hill for us?"

"Well, not too good," Mr. Bailey said. "You see, Doc Pulsifer can take the case to the Supreme Court, and so the whole thing is hanging in the air. For all we know the Supreme Court may rule out any telepathy in courts, and then we couldn't use Jenny as we planned. We'll just have to wait and see how things turn out, and that may take months."

"But we haven't *got* months!" Stanley said.

Mr. Bailey shifted uncomfortably in his seat. "I know. And I'm sorry it hasn't worked out, but there it is. It just took one ornery, stubborn old Yankee to spoil the thing. But cheer up. Jenny can still read minds anywhere but in court. We might as well look on the bright side of things."

Jenny pressed her face against the cold glass of the car window and didn't say anything. She had tried and tried and *nothing* had worked out. She couldn't keep the tears back, and so she pretended to look out the window and hoped nobody would notice.

CHAPTER EIGHTEEN

WHEN THEY REACHED the top of the hill they noticed a brown car with *U.S.A.* painted on it parked in front of the Pearson house. "What's that?" Stanley wondered.

"It looks like an army car," Joe said. "I wonder what the army wants."

"OK, kids," Mr. Bailey said. "Here's the end of the line. Time to get out. Mr. Bergamini and I have to get back to Springfield and report, so we'd better run along. Say thanks to your parents for us. Sorry we didn't have better luck."

They went in the back door a little cautiously. They had noticed that the family Plymouth was in the shed, and that meant their father was home early for some reason. They shut the door quietly behind them and walked out to the living room. There were two men in United States uniforms, with brass buttons and colored ribbons on the fronts of their jackets.

"Oh, hello there, children," Mr. Pearson said. "We were hoping you'd be back soon. This is Major Swanson, of the Army Intelligence, and this is Lieutenant Phipps. They came up here to bring us an important message from the Defense Department in Washington. It's about—well, perhaps you'd better tell them, Major."

The major squared his shoulders and looked firmly at them. "My orders were to tell you that the Defense Department has decided that this girl's telepathy is of importance to the national security and must be carefully protected. She is to be under guard in public at all times, and her telepathy is to be reserved for the Defense Department alone."

"Under guard?" Jenny repeated, her eyes open wide in surprise.

The major relaxed a little and smiled at her. "Oh, not when you're at home. Just when you go into town or to school and things like that."

"A guard in *school?*" Stanley said, hardly believing his ears. "You mean *soldiers?*"

"Just one soldier for the present," Major Swanson said. "He will accompany your sister to school and stay outside her classroom."

"Oh, wow!" Stanley said. "An armed guard! I wish I was in first grade."

"But what about the telepathy?" Joe said. "Can't we use Jenny to earn any more money?"

The major shook his head. "I'm afraid not, son. Her telepathy is too valuable to waste any of it. Your sister was recommended to us by a specialist in telepathy, and he said she was probably the only person in the country who could hear thoughts the way she could. Perhaps in the whole world, he said. Now when the Defense Department heard that, they had her declared a strategic resource and clamped a ban on her telepathy for anything but high priority use."

"But what about the *hill?*" Joe said, turning to Jenny and Stanley. "What can we do now?" He looked back at the major. "Would the Defense Department buy this hill for us? We can pay for almost half of it, and we've been using Jenny to try to get someone to buy the rest of it, and if you're going to keep us from using Jenny that way, wouldn't it be fair for you to put up the rest of the money?"

"Well, I . . . I don't know," Major Swanson said. "What you say sounds fair enough, but I don't think anything quite like this has come up before. How much money is needed?"

"Forty-three thousand dollars," Stanley said.

"That's too big for the petty cash account," the major said. "Anything over twenty thousand dollars has to be cleared with the Budget Bureau, and that takes a little time, you know. How long do you have?"

"Only nine days, until midnight April 15."

"Oh," the major said. "That's quite impossible. Nine days! The Defense Department has never done anything in nine days."

"But what will we *do*?" Stanley said desperately. "We've got to get *somebody* to put up the money, and if you stop Jenny's telepathy, how are we going to do it?"

"I don't know, son," the major said. "I'm sorry we've got to do this, but in the army orders are orders, and that's all there is to it."

"But how can Jenny stop her telepathy?" Joe wondered. "It just happens whenever she thinks about anybody, and sometimes she can't help it."

"Well," Major Swanson said, "I suppose we can't prevent a little mind reading going on around the house and just within the family, but there certainly shouldn't be any more communication outside of the family circle, and no long-distance stuff or anything like that to wear out the machinery."

Joe and Stanley looked at each other, and then they both looked at Jenny. For a while nobody in the room said anything.

"Well, that just about finishes it," Joe said, swallowing hard. "I guess there's not much more that we can do to save the hill."

Stanley jammed his hands into his pockets and walked over to the window. "We didn't have much hope left anyway, and now that's gone. We just don't have a chance now. I hope all those bulldozers sink out of sight in the *mud!*"

Jenny slipped into her mother's lap and buried her face in Mrs. Pearson's shoulder. Major Swanson stood up and straightened his jacket. "Ahem," he said, and looked around at the three children. Lieutenant Phipps stood behind him, turning his cap around in his hands. "Well," the major said, and straightened his jacket again. "I didn't realize how much this telepathy meant to you." He looked at the backs of the three children and hesitated. Lieutenant Phipps looked quite unhappy and got out a handkerchief and blew his nose.

"You see," Major Swanson said, "I thought this would be exciting news for you all. It isn't every family that can be of such a help to its country. I didn't know that you needed this telepathy so badly.

But it wasn't my idea, and I'm sorry if it upsets things for you."

"Oh, they don't blame you, Major," Mr. Pearson said. "It's just that they've tried terribly hard to keep this hill from being spoiled, and the luck's been running against them right along. It's been hard on them."

The major nodded. "Sure, I understand." He walked over to Joe and Stanley and patted them on the back. "It's tough when things aren't going your way, kids. But don't take it too hard. You had something worth fighting for, and you put up a good fight, and if you lost out it's nothing to be ashamed of."

He looked over at Jenny. "And your sister put up a good fight too," he said. "She doesn't have anything to be ashamed of either."

Jenny still kept her face hidden in her mother's shoulder, and the major and Lieutenant Phipps put on their coats. "Well," the major said, "I'll have the soldier report up here every morning before school, and remember not to go away from the house without him. You'll probably have some word from the Defense Department soon. Good-by."

When the two officers were gone, Mrs. Pearson started rushing about to get supper ready. Jenny set the table as usual, but she was very quiet and seemed to have her mind on something else, and she put all the forks on the right-hand side without noticing what she was doing.

Supper was unusually quiet that evening. By dessert time things were so gloomy that Mr. Pearson tried to cheer everybody up.

"Well, well," he said, "I guess that winds up the great hill project, so we might as well not fuss about it any more. You kids can have some good fun watching the bulldozers and power shovels working down there. I understand that they're going to bring in some big concrete culvert pipes about four feet thick and run the brook through them." He paused and nobody said anything. "It's going to be interesting watching them move those big pipes around."

The rest of the family were looking glumly at their Jello, and still nobody said anything.

"They'll probably have to use a crane, I should think," Mr. Pearson went on, but there was no response. "All right, all *right*," he said. "I give up. I guess nobody *wants* to cheer up right now. But Major Swanson was right. You kids have tried as hard as you could, and you don't have anything to be ashamed of."

At this Jenny groaned and buried her face in her napkin.

"Why, what's the matter, Jenny?" her mother asked. "Are you sick?"

Jenny shook her head. "I *have* done something to be ashamed of," she said through her napkin. "I shouldn't have taken all that money for that quiz show in New York. I shouldn't ever have *been* in the quiz show. It was all a fake. I was *cheating.* And that's why everything has gone wrong ever since. It's all my fault."

Mrs. Pearson rested her hand on Jenny's shoulder. "Now Jenny," she said, "if that's the way you feel about it, you can send the money right back to the broadcasting company, and then everything will be all right again."

Joe and Stanley looked dismayed at this, but they didn't say anything. Jenny lifted her face from her napkin. "*Can* I do that?" she said hopefully.

"But—" Stanley said, and stopped.

"Of course you can," Mrs. Pearson said, looking across at her husband. "Can't she, Ed?"

"Why, yes, we haven't spent a penny of it. She can send it all back. She'd probably better send it back if she feels that way about it."

"Oh, good," Jenny said. "I want to send it back right away. Tonight."

"Now wait a minute," her father said. "I'll have to go down and speak to the bank about withdrawing all that hundred thousand dollars again. I'm going to be pretty busy with a shipment of lumber tomorrow and the next day. But I can go down to Westfield on Thursday. Would that be soon enough?"

Jenny's face fell. "But I want to do it *now*. Then I can forget all about it, and everything will be all right again."

"I have an idea," Joe said. "Why don't we send off a letter to the broadcasting company tonight and explain things to them, and then we can send them the money later."

"That sounds good," Mr. Pearson said. "And it might be a good idea to give them some warning. We probably should wait to hear from them before we ship off all that money. Is that all right, Jenny?"

Jenny nodded and put her napkin back in her lap.

After supper Jenny figured out what she wanted to say in her letter and dictated it to Joe, who wrote it down for her. It went like this:

Dear North American Broadcasting Corporation:
Ever since I won the TV quiz contest and the hundred thousand dollars I didn't feel right about it because I think it wasn't quite fair the way I won it because I didn't really know the answers

to all the questions I just heard them in my head when I listened to the quizmaster thinking and that's why I want to send back the hundred thousand dollars as soon as you say OK and then I will feel better about it and I hope you will understand.

Yours truly,

JENNY PEARSON

Joe felt a little uneasy about having it all one sentence that way, but that was the way Jenny said it, and besides she signed her name at the bottom, so everyone would know it was her letter and not his. They put it in an envelope and addressed it and put a stamp on it, and put it in their father's overcoat pocket so he would mail it in the morning when he went past the post office.

The next morning was Tuesday, and the soldier came up to the house while they were still eating breakfast, and Mrs. Pearson had him come in and have a cup of coffee with them. His name was Bruce MacLeod, and he had red hair when he took off his cap. He leaned his rifle up against the dining room wall, and Joe and Stanley looked at him with great respect. After breakfast Private MacLeod and the three children walked down the road together, and Mrs. Pearson watched out the kitchen window until they were out of sight.

It was quite a sensation to have a soldier in school. He took up his post outside the first grade classroom, but so many children kept getting excused to go to the bathroom or to get a drink of water so they could get a glimpse of the soldier that Mr. Billings decided it would be better if the soldier stayed inside the classroom instead. This suited Private MacLeod better too, because by lunchtime he was pretty bored with standing out in the hall. Miss Romaine gave him an empty desk to sit at, and of course it was miles too small for him, but he stuck his knees out on each side of it and was pretty comfortable.

He was a little embarrassed at first because he wasn't used to being in first grade like that, but by Wednesday he felt more at home, and Miss Romaine said that since they were studying about America it would be nice if he told the class all about the Army, and he did. He told them all about basic training and kitchen detail and what a private first class was. And the whole class got to be good friends with him and he helped them with their subtraction and took charge of the fast reading group so Miss Romaine could work with the others. He was a big help to the class and he kept his rifle in the corner of the room and wouldn't let anybody touch it.

Thursday evening Mr. Watson stopped in at the Pearsons'. His black hair was slicked back and he didn't take off his overcoat. "I just wanted to explain what I was going to do," he said. "If the weather stays dry like this for another four or five days, the ground will be hard enough to drive a truck on, and I'm going to have them truck in the big concrete pipes and unload them down by the brook next Monday or Tuesday. Now Monday's only the thirteenth of April, and I know your option to buy the hill runs until the sixteenth. I told you the sixteenth and I'll stick by it, and if you should have the money by midnight on the fifteenth, the hill is yours, and I'll take the culverts out again. The way things look, though, there isn't much chance that you'll have the money, so I didn't think you'd mind if I went ahead with unloading the pipes, so I won't have to lose time later on. It's just a practical arrangement, and I wanted to tell you so you wouldn't be surprised on Monday or Tuesday when the trucks come in."

"Well, thanks," Mr. Pearson said. "When does the power shovel start in?"

"Eight o'clock on the morning of the sixteenth," Mr. Watson said, rubbing his hands together. "The construction company is all primed to begin the first thing after your option runs out. It'll be a big day. You won't recognize the place after they get through."

"Probably not," Mr. Pearson said.

Mr. Watson put on his stiff black felt hat. "Well, I've got to run along. Good-by."

CHAPTER NINETEEN

THE NEXT DAY was Friday and it was a beautiful spring day and the forsythia outside the school building was in full bloom and the first graders could hardly wait until recess time came and they could go outside to play. Private MacLeod had been teaching them how to play softball, and even the girls were learning.

Every now and then Miss Romaine would stare out the window at the green grass and soft clouds and she would forget where she was and a wistful look would come over her face, and then the children would begin to notice and start whispering and that would wake her up and she would go back to the arithmetic facts.

Just before school was over Lieutenant Phipps took Private MacLeod out in the hall to talk to him about having another soldier take his place for the next week. Jenny was waiting for them to finish talking, and all the other children had left. Miss Romaine called Jenny over to her desk.

"Are you allowed to do any mind reading at all now, Jenny?"

"The major said I could only do it just in the family," Jenny said, looking down at her feet as she answered.

"Would you consider—that is, do you call your Uncle Harold part of the family?"

"Oh, yes," Jenny said.

"Well," Miss Romaine said, "could you tell me how he feels about—" She stopped and looked anxiously toward the door.

"About what?" Jenny said.

"About *me*," Miss Romaine said in a low voice. "I mean, is he still angry at what I said to him at that sliding party at your house at New Year's?"

"Oh," Jenny said. She looked at Miss Romaine curiously, and then she looked away and began running her finger along the edge of the desk. "I'll try to find out," she said. She turned her head and seemed to listen. They could hear Lieutenant Phipps's voice out in the hall. He said something about E Company.

"All right," Jenny said at last. She kept on running her finger along the edge of the desk and didn't look at Miss Romaine at all. "Uncle Harold isn't angry about what you said. He likes you. I think he wants to invite you out to supper sometime, but he doesn't dare ask you."

Miss Romaine's face lighted up, and she smiled. "Is your uncle that shy?"

Jenny nodded, still keeping her eyes on her finger. "Oh, yes, he's awfully shy." Just then Private Mac-Leod walked into the classroom to get his gun.

"I won't keep her any longer," Miss Romaine called out to him. "Now be sure to study that spelling, Jenny." Jenny looked at her in surprise, and she thought she saw Miss Romaine wink at her.

Saturday morning Private MacLeod came in during breakfast and announced that he was going to stay on the job another week. He liked it so much in Pearson's Corners that he asked the lieutenant to let him stay on instead of being replaced. He helped with the housecleaning in the morning and when the children went down the hill to the brook after lunch he went with them. Of course he had to go wherever Jenny went, but he didn't seem to mind.

It was a warm day for April, and they went wading in the brook. Teddy Watson came down later, and he fell in as usual, but Private MacLeod fished him out and had him spread out his shirt in the sun, and then made him run around until he had dried off.

"Are you going to like moving to Florida?" they asked Teddy Watson. "You can go in swimming all year around there probably."

Teddy shook his head. "I don't want to go to Florida. I want to stay here. It's just Pop that wants to move to Florida. He says it's no good staying in a little town like this all the time. He wants us to live somewhere where people are really *living*. He says it's too cramped here in Pearson's Corners."

"But you want to stay here?" Joe asked.

"I sure do. I'd give anything to have something happen so we couldn't move away. But I don't suppose it will."

Uncle Harold came for Sunday dinner. He said it was a shame that the hill was going to be lost after all. He had thought at first that with Jenny's wonderful ear they were sure to win out, but the luck had been against them.

After dinner Uncle Harold went outside to tighten up a hose connection in the engine of his pickup truck. Jenny came out and watched him, because it was Joe's and Stanley's turn to do the dishes, and she didn't have anything to do. She sat on the fender and peered under the hood.

"You haven't been up to see us much since New Year's, Uncle Harold."

"Been pretty busy this winter, Jenny." He loosened the clamp and shoved the hose higher on the connection. "By the way, Jenny, can you still do any mind-reading jobs, or is that illegal?"

"They let me do little ones in the family," Jenny said. "Why?"

"I wondered if you'd do a little one for me," Uncle Harold said. "But you've got to promise first that you won't tell anyone."

"I'll promise," Jenny said.

"Good." Uncle Harold pulled his head out from under the hood and looked toward the house. "Now where's that soldier?"

"He's in the house," Jenny said. "He just looks out every now and then to make sure I'm all right. He won't bother us."

"Well, what I wanted you to do was to listen in on —you're sure you won't tell on me?"

"I promised, didn't I?"

"OK. I'll trust you," Uncle Harold said. "Now look, could you listen in on Miss Romaine and find

252

out if she's still sore at me for what I said about her here at New Year's?"

"Miss Romaine?" Jenny sounded almost surprised. "All right, I'll listen." She put her head on one side and sat on the fender without saying anything.

Uncle Harold finished tightening up the connection and put the screwdriver back in the car. Then he came back and watched Jenny with a worried look. After a while Jenny nodded to herself.

"Well?" Uncle Harold said impatiently. "What's the answer?"

"Pretty good," Jenny said, swinging her feet and looking over toward the kitchen door. "She doesn't seem to be sore at you at all. As a matter of fact, it sounds as if she wouldn't mind being invited out to supper sometime. Then you could both explain that you weren't sore at each other."

"Jeepers, why should I be sore at *her?*" Uncle Harold said. He put down the hood, and then leaned his elbows on it. "You sure you heard it right? How do you know it was me she was thinking about? Maybe it was that soldier boy."

"Nope, it was you," Jenny said. "I heard your name as plain as anything. *Harold*—just like that." She slid off the fender and ran into the house. When

she looked out the window Uncle Harold was still leaning his elbows on the hood of the truck.

Monday morning the sun was shining in a clear sky. "No rain today, I guess," Mr. Pearson said. "Those culverts will probably be in today or tomorrow."

When Jenny went up to the teacher's desk to have her subtraction examples corrected, Miss Romaine whispered to her, "You were right, Jenny. He *did* invite me out to supper. For tonight."

The next day was gray and cloudy in the morning. Three big trailer trucks came past the school, each with twelve concrete culvert pipes, and they went over the bridge and turned off the road and drove over the meadow along the brook. Then the crew of men unloaded the pipes by rolling them off the trucks on heavy timbers. One of the culverts rolled down the bank into the brook and stood up on end, like a small tower. By the middle of the afternoon the men were finished and they drove the trucks away, leaving deep tracks in the meadow.

Just about the time the trucks left it began to rain. It was too wet to go to the meadow and look at the culverts, so all the school children went home instead, with their coat collars turned up to keep out the wet. It rained all that night in a soft steady drizzle, and it rained all the next day. "Watson sure was lucky with the weather," Mr. Pearson said at supper. "That meadow is almost a swamp by now. You couldn't even get a wheelbarrow in there today."

The next day was Wednesday, April 15. "This is the last day," Mr. Pearson said at breakfast. "I must say I admire the way you kids are taking your disappointment. At least it isn't coming as a sudden blow, anyway. We've had a little time to get braced for it. I understand Watson is going to have the power shovel standing right on the edge of the meadow, so it'll be all ready to go into action the first thing tomorrow. We'd all better take our last look at the old brook, because it won't ever be the same again."

There was a long silence, and finally Mrs. Pearson straightened up and put on a cheerful look. "Here, won't someone eat this last piece of toast? More milk, Joe? Jenny, I'm surprised we haven't heard from the broadcasting company. Your letter went off ten days ago."

Stanley helped himself to the toast. "They probably took one look at the letter and dropped dead with surprise. I bet no one else ever wanted to send back the money like that."

That afternoon the power shovel arrived on a big trailer. The weather was still pretty damp, but the school children stood around watching while the shovel operator drove down the ramp off the trailer, with the caterpillar treads clanking against the planks. He moved the machine just off the road and rested the big steel bucket on the ground, as if it was waiting to take a big bite of the green sod. He swung down from the cab.

"Are you going to cover up the brook?" Andy Zwillinger asked him.

"Sure thing, kid. Somebody leaves these brooks lying around, and we cover 'em up. That's progress. Now look here, you kids," he said, taking off his leather gloves. "I've locked the cab, so there's no use trying to get in. And I don't want nobody climbing on this shovel and getting hurt. Understand?" He climbed into the trailer truck and drove away. The power shovel looked big standing there all by itself. It was painted orange and on its side it had ROVINOSO & SONS in great black letters.

When everyone had gone home, Jenny walked along the side of the brook. This was the last time, because tomorrow the shovel would rip up the ground and scatter mud and stones over the meadow, and they would put in the pipes and cover them up and then there would be no more brook. She wondered if sometimes she would come down here again among the houses and driveways that would be here and kneel down and put her ear to the ground—either ear, it didn't matter—and if she listened very hard, would she be able to hear the water flowing down underneath?

Private MacLeod followed her, but not very closely. He was a very understanding sort of guard and knew when people wanted to be alone. Jenny walked along the brook, which was rushing noisily over the stones. The afternoon was getting late, and there was a gray mist on the meadow. It was growing dark, and soon she would have to go home to supper, but first she would have to walk along the brook all the way to the edge of the meadow and that would be her good-by forever.

The culverts loomed up gray out of the mist. The one that was standing on end in the brook was making the water flow around it on both sides with a rushing sound. Some one had propped a pole up against the culvert, perhaps to keep it from tipping over. She walked to the edge of the meadow through the mist and the twilight, and then stood and watched where the water flowed under the barbed wire fence and rushed away into the woods where it was too dark to see. It was sad to see it rushing away like that.

She gave a little shiver because it was growing chilly, and then she turned to go up the hill. High up above her the lights of her house were fuzzy through the mist. As she climbed the hill the sound of the brook faded away behind her.

After supper there was a telephone call from Mrs. Watson. Had they seen anything of Teddy Watson? He hadn't come home to supper. His father was out looking for him now.

None of the Pearson family had seen him. "He wasn't down at the power shovel with the rest of us," Stanley said. "I thought he went right home after school."

Mrs. Watson hung up, but just a few minutes later Mr. Hagerty called. "Hello, Ed," he said. "Watson was just in to see me and he's plenty worried about that boy of his. He's looked all over and hasn't seen a trace of him anywhere. So I told him we'd all pitch in and search the whole town. I've got some men assigned to this end of town, and if you take your hillside, I'll have Zwillinger and LaBonte check on the brook, and Billings can take a bunch of men down into the woods. If he's found we'll ring the church bell to call in the search parties. We'll all plan to meet back at the bridge in an hour, OK?"

"OK," Mr. Pearson said and hung up. "Joe and Stanley, get your flashlights. We'll start at the top of the hill and work down."

"Can I come too?" Jenny asked, but not very hopefully.

"I'm afraid not, Jenny," her father said. "We'll have to move pretty fast. You'd be more of a hindrance than a help."

The three men of the family walked out into the dark. Jenny watched the long beams of their flashlights in the mist. Here and there all over the town she could see lights moving. Private MacLeod called to see if Jenny was staying at home.

"Fine," he said. "You keep her there, and I'll be able to help look for this boy."

Jenny and her mother kept listening for the church bell, but an hour passed without any sound. The searchers all gathered at the bridge, and then spread out again to cover the outlying sections of town. Jenny could see the lights moving about high on the hills.

"Jenny, you'll have to go to bed," her mother told her. "It's quarter to ten."

"Oh, Mommy, I *can't* go to sleep if Teddy Watson is still lost."

"Well, go up and put on your pajamas, and then I'll let you sit up a while longer."

Jenny wrapped up in a blanket and sat on a chair in front of the window. The two of them watched the moving lights anxiously.

Then the front door burst open and Mr. Watson hurried in. His hair was down in front of his eyes and he was breathing hard. His coat sleeve was torn and he was all mud up to his knees.

"Jenny!" he said. "You've got to help me. We've looked all over and can't find him. Can you *listen* for him? If you can hear him thinking it might give us something to go on. Can you try?"

Jenny looked at him in dismay. "But I—" She stopped. "I'll try," she said in a small voice. She put her head down on her arms on the window sill and stayed very still. She tried and tried as hard as she could, but nothing came. Just silence, except for Mr. Watson's heavy breathing.

261

Suddenly she had a thought. She lifted her head. "Have you looked in the culverts?"

Mr. Watson nodded. "Yes. All of them."

"Even the one that's standing up?"

"He couldn't get into that one. It's too high."

"But he could!" Jenny insisted. "Look in that one!"

Mr. Watson shrugged his shoulders. "I'll try *anything*," he said in a desperate voice. "Even if it's hopeless."

When he was gone they watched out the window some more and for a long time there was nothing, and then they saw a light down at the bottom of the meadow and it moved around awhile and then it began waving back and forth and some other lights moved toward it, and then in a very short time the church bell began ringing and it rang and rang and it was a wonderful sound in the darkness.

Her mother turned toward her with tears in her eyes. "Oh, Jenny, you're a little hero!" she said, and hugged her very tight. She got out a handkerchief and blew her nose. "Oh, dear, it's almost eleven o'clock," she said. "Now, Jenny, off to bed right away. Quick!"

CHAPTER TWENTY

MR. PEARSON bowed his head over the Sunday roast chicken.

"Ahem," he said. "Let us give thanks for this beautiful spring day, and for the green grass that's coming up on the meadow, and for the brook that's *still* flowing at the bottom of the hill"—here he paused to breathe in the steam rising from the roast chicken—"and for the wonderful smell of this bird—"

"And for our two nice guests," Mrs. Pearson added, smiling at Uncle Harold and Miss Romaine.

"And for the way Jenny found where Teddy Watson was Wednesday night," Joe said. "Maybe Mr. Watson will give us a reward for that."

"And for Teddy Watson getting *lost* when he did," Stanley said. "Right on the fifteenth of April. If he waited another—"

263

"That makes today the nineteenth of April," Joe said. "Paul Revere day."

" 'Listen my children and you shall hear,' " Stanley muttered, his eyes fixed on the mashed potatoes, " 'of the midnight ride of—' "

"Now just a minute," Mr. Pearson said. "I'm the one who's supposed to say grace around here, and I object when other people are always interrupting me to—"

"Look out!" Stanley said. "You almost tipped over your water."

Mr. Pearson moved his glass toward the center of the table. "Now what was I talking about?"

"Perhaps you'd better start carving while you talk," Mrs. Pearson suggested. "The food will be all cold if we don't start in."

"What was Mr. Watson saying to you after church?" Joe asked.

"Oh, yes!" Mr. Pearson said, plunging the carving knife into the plump chicken. "That's the big news! I was saving it until we were all together."

"Excuse me," Miss Romaine said. "Is Jenny all right?" She looked across the table at Jenny, who was still sitting with her hands folded and her head bowed.

"Daddy hasn't said amen yet," Jenny said. "He *never* remembers."

"Oh, yes," Mr. Pearson said. "Amen." He paused while he twisted off the drumstick. "Now for the announcement. Mr. Watson came up to me after church and shook my hand and said that Jenny had saved his son's life and they would never forget it. Then he told me that he had called off the power shovel—that was why they didn't start digging Thursday morning—and that he was going to get those culverts hauled away as soon as the ground was dry again, and he's *not* going to sell the hill for house lots, but he's already arranged with the selectmen to turn over the whole hill and the brook to the town to be kept just the way it is. And he also said that he'd been thinking things over and he decided that any town that would turn out that way and help a man when he was in trouble was too good a place to leave, and so he's giving up his idea of going to Florida, and he's going to stay right on in Pearson's Corners. Well, that's the announcement, and I guess the old hill is going to be saved after all."

Joe and Stanley got up and danced around the table, whooping and stamping until the water started to spill out of the glasses. Jenny didn't say

anything, but her eyes were shining, and you could tell how she felt just by looking at her.

When things had quieted down a little, Uncle Harold looked across the table at Miss Romaine. He took a swallow of water and stuck his finger inside his collar to loosen it and then he said, "I've got a little announcement to make too." He took another swallow of water. "Miss Romaine and I are —that is, she—well, what I mean is, we're going to be married."

"Why *Harold!*" Mrs. Pearson said. "What a surprise! So *that's* why you wanted me to invite Miss Romaine here for Sunday dinner. I thought it was just so you could get to *know* her! Well, well, you managed to keep your secret very well. I haven't heard a word about it from anyone, not even Eunice LaBonte, and *she* knows everything that's going on."

"We didn't know ourselves until just a little while ago," Uncle Harold said. "I guess these things just suddenly happen."

"You made a very good choice, Harold," Mr. Pearson said. "Miss Romaine is the best sledder on our school faculty."

"Why, Jenny, what's the matter?" Mrs. Pearson said. "You look so sad."

"If Miss Romaine goes away," Jenny said, "who will we have for a teacher?"

"But I'm not going away, Jenny," Miss Romaine said.

"That's the other part of my announcement," Uncle Harold went on. "I'm going to sell my business in Southwick to a fellow that's been trying to buy it, and I'm going to start a business here in Pearson's Corners. You know, refrigerators, radios, television sets and things like that. I figured that this town was going to grow in the next few years, and I thought it would be a good place to set up in. And so, Miss Romaine can go on teaching at the school."

"You mean you're going to live right here in town?" Stanley said. "That will be neat."

"And furthermore," Uncle Harold went on, "I'm going to need some assistants at my store. Some young fellows who know a little something about electronics. Any idea where I can get two helpers like that?"

"Right here!" Stanley and Joe both said at once.

"Well, that's fine," Uncle Harold said. "I'll be able to use you after school in the afternoons, and on Saturdays too probably. I wouldn't be surprised if it brought you a tidy little income. Of course nothing like the hundred thousand dollars that Jenny made on television. By the way, if Watson is giving the hill to the town, Jenny will have all the money left, won't she? How much will there be after taxes? Thirty-two thousand dollars, wasn't it?"

"Oh, we're going to send that all back to the broadcasting company," Joe said. "Jenny didn't feel right about it, because she thinks the mind reading wasn't fair on a quiz program."

"Oh," Uncle Harold said. "I didn't know."

Stanley helped himself to more gravy on his mashed potatoes. "Anyway," he said, "what's so great about thirty-two thousand dollars? When the government begins using Jenny's telepathy, she'll have *plenty* of money."

Jenny stirred uneasily at this and looked uncomfortable.

"Oh, that reminds me," Mr. Pearson said. He got up and went out into the living room and came back with a letter in his hand. "I got this at the post office yesterday, but there was so much going on that I forgot all about it. It's for you, Jenny."

Everybody watched while Jenny opened up the envelope. She took out the letter and unfolded it, but it was too hard reading, so she passed it to Joe to read out loud.

April 15

Dear Jenny Pearson:

I am sorry not to have answered your letter sooner, but I was away on a trip, and have just read it this morning when I came back to the office. I understand your feelings about the prize money, but since you have been honest with me, I will be honest with you. Your appearance on our program was the biggest thing that ever happened to us, and because of it we have become the most successful company in the business.

Now with all the help you have given us, we certainly wouldn't feel quite right to allow you to send back the prize money that you won on our program. After all, you were giving a performance that no one else in the world could match, and so we think you deserve the prize. So please don't think of sending it back to us.

Sincerely,

Samuel R. Heavyside, *President*

"Aha!" Stanley said. "They want you to *keep* it, Jenny. So you have thirty-two thousand dollars after all. What are you going to buy with it? Let's start by getting TV sets for every room in the house. Then we could—"

"I don't think so," Jenny said. "I think I'll keep the money for another emergency."

"Well, anyway," Stanley went on, "that money's just a start, because the government will pay you *thousands* for your telepathy, because of course it's the only one in the whole world, so I think we could hold out for a thousand dollars a week—or maybe more—and that would be fifty-two thousand dollars a year, and—"

"No," Jenny said suddenly.

"No?" Stanley looked blank.

"I'm not going to," Jenny said. "I can't do it."

"Can't *do* it?" Stanley repeated. "Why not?"

"I just *can't*, that's all."

Joe looked at her closely. "You mean you can't hear thoughts any more? Is that it, Jenny?"

She nodded.

"Shucks!" Stanley said. "And we were only just beginning to get this thing going. Think what a future we could have had."

"We weren't either just beginning," Jenny said. "We went a long way, and it was much too far, *I* think. I didn't like all that *listening* to people that way, and it made me feel all wrong every time I did it. And it got worse and worse as I went along, and I'm *glad* I can't do it any more. I can hear all I want to the way I am now."

"There, there, Jenny," her mother said. "Don't

get all worked up about it. It's all over now, anyway, and everything will be all right again."

"That's OK, Jenny," Joe told her. "The Jenny Pearson Private Ear and Long Distance Listening Service is now closing down, and Stanley and I are resigning as your managers and we're going into Electrical Service and Repairs. After all, it was good fun while it lasted, but we couldn't expect it to go on forever."

"Yeah, I suppose that's right," Stanley agreed. "And anyway, we wouldn't have time for private work if we went into business with Uncle Harold. But Jenny, when did you stop? After you located Teddy Watson?"

Jenny shook her head. "Before that. The last time I heard any thoughts was that day in Boston, when I was listening to Doc Pulsifer, and he said he didn't blame me for listening, because I was just doing what I was told and didn't know any better. When he said that, there was a little pop in my ear just like when you get water in your ear when you're in swimming. And after that I couldn't hear any more thoughts. But I didn't want to tell anybody because I thought maybe I could still help save the hill somehow."

Joe looked puzzled. "But Jenny, how did you find

where Teddy Watson was, then? We all thought you'd heard him thinking."

"I didn't hear him at all," Jenny said. "But I *thought* about him, and suddenly I remembered that I had seen a pole leaning against that culvert, and then I thought it was just the kind of thing that Teddy Watson would do, to climb up the pole and jump down inside and then not be able to climb out again. It just came to me, that's all."

Stanley grinned. "I wonder what the Defense Department's going to think when they find out that they've had a soldier guarding something all this time when it wasn't there at all. And Private Mac-Leod was wasting all his time sitting there in first grade. I'll bet he'll be sore when he hears that."

"From what *I've* heard," Mrs. Pearson said, "he wasn't wasting his time at all. He was busy helping out with the teaching. Isn't that right, Miss Romaine?"

"Yes, indeed," Miss Romaine said with a smile. "He's been a big help. But of course it isn't really what he was trained for, and I don't suppose either the school or the Army would want him there as a regular thing. They're really not in the same line of work."

All this while Uncle Harold had been looking

curiously at Jenny, as if he were trying to figure out something. Finally there was a lull in the talking.

"There's something I don't understand here," he said slowly. "You said that you stopped hearing any thoughts the day you went to Boston. Is that right?"

"Yes, Uncle Harold," Jenny said. There was a kind of expectant look in her eyes, as if she knew what was coming.

"And when was it you went to Boston?"

"On Monday."

"But *what* Monday?"

"That was Monday, April 6," Joe said. "I remember from the telegram."

"Monday, April 6," Uncle Harold repeated slowly. "*Sixth!* Why, that was two weeks ago! You mean you haven't been hearing any thoughts since *then?*"

"No, Uncle Harold," Jenny said, looking right at him. Everyone was watching them with great interest, but Miss Romaine was the most interested of all.

"Well, then," Uncle Harold said, "you couldn't have been hearing any thoughts last Sunday, could you?"

"No, Uncle Harold. I couldn't hear any thoughts."

Uncle Harold was all confused. "But if you couldn't hear any thoughts—how could you—when

I asked you—well, you remember what I *asked* you, don't you?"

"Yes," Jenny said sweetly. "You asked me if—"

"Never MIND!" Uncle Harold said quickly. "You don't need to tell me. I *know* what I asked you. But what I *don't* know is how you could have answered my question. That is, how you could have answered it *right*."

Miss Romaine's mouth twitched a little at the corners, but she didn't say anything.

"Well, I'll tell you," Jenny said. She looked around the table, and they were all looking at her with great curiosity and even Stanley had stopped eating and the sunshine was flooding in the dining room window, and suddenly she felt perfectly happy for the first time in months. "I'll tell you. You don't have to have tape recorders and microphones or even a special kind of ear like mine. If you just *know* people well enough, and *like* them well enough, you can find out all you need to know."